"Lila…"

Zach said her name in that husky tone he'd used last night when he'd kissed her by the bay, and she looked up into those eyes of his, waiting and wanting so much from him. She'd always told herself she was bold and that she had the life she wanted, but she also knew that she'd been afraid to take any risks.

This was the riskiest thing she'd ever done. Kissing a famous bad boy on his private plane…this wasn't the Lila Jones she'd always been.

And that brush of his lips against hers was sending chills through her. He put his hands on her waist and lifted her, pulling her onto his lap. She wrapped her arm around his shoulders as he deepened the kiss, his tongue brushing over hers.

This was changing from doing something risky to doing something she'd always wanted but had never been able to do…

* * *

The Trouble with Bad Boys
by Katherine Garbera is part of the
Texas Cattleman's Club: Heir Apparent series.

Dear Reader,

Happy May! I'm so excited to be contributing to the Texas Cattleman's Club again. I totally love a bad boy hero and I had so much fun writing Zach. He has all the confidence, arrogance and swagger that you could want, but he tempers it with both humor and humility.

He meets his match in Lila Jones. She's smart, feisty, funny, totally comfortable in her own skin but also maybe wishes she were a little more daring. Zach sort of challenges her and brings out a side to Lila that she never expected to like as much as she does.

Both of them fight falling for each other because they live two very different lives and finding a way for any relationship between them to be more than just a fling is difficult for them to see. But they make each other look at their own worlds and the larger world with different eyes.

I hope you enjoy reading their story!

Happy reading!

Katherine

KATHERINE GARBERA

THE TROUBLE WITH BAD BOYS

Thanks to Stacy Boyd for her insightful edits
on this book, making it really shine.

Special thanks and acknowledgment are given
to Katherine Garbera for her contribution to the
Texas Cattleman's Club: Heir Apparent miniseries.

HARLEQUIN®

DESIRE™

Recycling programs
for this product may
not exist in your area.

ISBN-13: 978-1-335-23288-5

The Trouble with Bad Boys

Copyright © 2021 by Harlequin Books S.A.

This edition published by arrangement with Harlequin Books S.A.

For questions and comments about the quality of this book,
please contact us at CustomerService@Harlequin.com.

Harlequin Enterprises ULC
22 Adelaide St. West, 40th Floor
Toronto, Ontario M5H 4E3, Canada
www.Harlequin.com

Printed in U.S.A.

Katherine Garbera is the *USA TODAY* bestselling author of more than ninety-five books. Her writing is known for its emotional punch and sizzling sensuality. She lives in the Midlands of the UK with the love of her life; her son, who recently graduated university; and a spoiled miniature dachshund. You can find her online at www.katherinegarbera.com and on Facebook, Twitter and Instagram.

Books by Katherine Garbera

Harlequin Desire

The Wild Caruthers Bachelors

Tycoon Cowboy's Baby Surprise
The Tycoon's Fiancée Deal
Craving His Best Friend's Ex

One Night

One Night with His Ex
One Night, Two Secrets
One Night to Risk It All
Her One Night Proposal

Texas Cattleman's Club: Heir Apparent

The Trouble with Bad Boys

Visit her Author Profile page at Harlequin.com, or katherinegarbera.com, for more titles.

You can also find Katherine Garbera on Facebook, along with other Harlequin Desire authors, at Facebook.com/harlequindesireauthors!

This book is dedicated to my wild, crazy family
who kept me sane with weekly family video chats.
Rob, Courtney, Lucas & Georgina, Tabby,
Josh & Darcey, and Bobby & Brooke. Love you!

One

Lila Jones looked at her phone for the hundredth time as if she could magically will a big-name Instagrammer to respond to her request. It wasn't working. If she weren't such a people pleaser, she never would have volunteered to do a task that was so obviously outside of her wheelhouse.

After all, she was a classic girl next door with her unhighlighted long brown hair, thick bangs and a tortoiseshell barrette that kept the sides off her face. She dressed for comfort rather than style and was totally okay with that. Men always wanted to be her friend and confide things to her. Women liked her, *genuinely* liked her, because she was never going to compete with them for attention once they were all in a room.

She loved that about herself. *Honestly.* But she'd volunteered to get some high-profile social media influencer interested in *Soiree on the Bay, the luxury food, art and wine festival* being held on Appaloosa Island, located about three hours from Royal, Texas. But the truth was, despite her good intentions, she wasn't someone that a famous social media personality was going to respond to. Pictures of Whiskers, her elderly friend Winifred's cat, and her favorite books stacked up by her cup of Earl Grey had garnered the usual seven likes by her parents and some of their friends and the Royal Chamber of Commerce account that she managed. And that was it. She wasn't bringing anything exciting or relevant to the table.

She had her planner open in front of her, jotting notes as she sipped her iced coffee. While she knew it was going to be an uphill battle, she wasn't going to fail at this. Because more than anything, Lila didn't want to let the committee down. In fact, that was one thing in her wheelhouse: she was dependable. She opened her social media direct messages and her heart leaped to her throat when she saw that Zach Benning had read her message. Wow. *Seriously?* Although she'd known it was a long shot, she had optimistically added the address of the chamber of commerce and an invite for him to drop in whenever.

Then she saw that he had given the message a thumbs-up.

What did that mean?

Was he going to come to Royal?

He wasn't her top choice of influencer to help promote their event because he was a little too wild—favoring fast cars and women over sensible ones. She had hoped they'd get someone they could rely on. But still…if he did show up and he tweeted or posted one thing, they'd probably get a million likes and that would really help to give the festival world-wide attention.

Now she needed to sweeten the deal. But how? She clicked on his image and tried to ignore the fact that his bright blue eyes were smiling intriguingly at her…well, not at *her*. At anyone who clicked on his profile, Lila noted. He was, after all, all about his image. And that photo screamed, *look at me and my fabulous life.*

Hmm. How could she use that to her advantage?

Billy Holmes had said that Royal was an undiscovered gem. And that Soiree on the Bay was just the first step to getting more influencers and money into their town. She wasn't sure that Zach or any other influencer would see it that way. Because as sophisticated as some of the residents of Royal were, it was still a small town in Texas, and Appaloosa Island was remote… Perfect for a Coachella-type event, but she was going to have to convince them of that.

Direct message to Zach Benning:

@Zach You've probably seen everything and been everywhere, but I guarantee you've never experienced anything like the southern glam of Royal, Texas. The Soiree is just one small part of what we have to offer. Drop me a DM soon. You're our first choice, but there are a lot of others waiting to—

"Hey, Lila. It sure is hot here today. Do you mind if I join you for a minute? I'm waiting for my take-out order."

She glanced up to see Charlotte Jarrett. Charlotte was a renowned chef and was working on the advisory committee for the Soiree along with Lila. Charlotte had been living in Los Angeles and recently returned to Royal and reconnected with her baby daddy, Ross Edmond Jr. That had caused a bit of a scandal around town and Rusty had gone so far as to disown his own son over the incident.

"Not at all. I could actually use your input on this text… I'm trying to up the ante and get Zach Benning to our town."

"Let me see what you've got," Charlotte said.

Lila pushed her phone across the table, and as the other woman read the message, she heard the roar of a powerful sports car coming down Main Street. Looking up, she saw it pull to an abrupt stop in front of the chamber of commerce building, directly across from the coffee shop where she and Charlotte were sitting.

As soon as the cherry-red Ferrari came to a halt, a tall blonde woman hopped out of the convertible, slamming the door so hard that in a less luxurious car, the vehicle would have rocked.

"You're a total asshole!" she fumed. "I hope you rot in this Podunk town. Because I'm not the only one done with you. LA is, too."

The blonde stalked away from the car in impossibly high heels at a furious pace that Lila had to admire. If she were wearing heels that tall she'd have probably twisted her ankle.

"Wow. You don't see that every day."

"No, you certainly don't," Lila agreed. "I wonder who is driving…kind of reminds me of something Rusty might do."

"Ha. You're not wrong," Charlotte said.

Lila chuckled, glancing back over at the car as a tall man emerged from behind the wheel. He put on his sunglasses, running one hand through his thick brown hair, and it fell immediately back into place. Leaving him looking artfully ruffled.

Her gaze raked over him, taking him in from head to toe. He wore jeans and a skintight designer T-shirt that showed off his muscled chest and biceps. Sheesh. The dude looked like he hadn't missed a date at the gym—ever. Honestly, if he went to her gym she knew she would be there every day, too. Probably just to stare at him.

He was hotter than the May heat surrounding them on this Texas afternoon. He moved as if he had all the time in the world…like he knew all eyes were on him. She'd never in her life walked with that much confidence.

He moved toward them with intent.

Don't be silly, Lila, he's walking to the coffee shop.

She forced herself to look back at her friend. "What do you think? Should I send it?"

"Uh, no. I don't think you will need to do that," Charlotte said.

She was staring over Lila's shoulder toward the Ferrari and Mr. Hottie.

The closer he got, the easier it was to see his trademark dark sunglasses, and there was no mistaking that cut physique. OMG. It was Zach Benning.

Well then.

The waitress called Charlotte's name for her to-go order. "Let me know how this goes."

She left the table. Lila wondered if Zach was going to stop and see her or go to the chamber of commerce first. But he surveyed everyone sitting outside, his attention focused on Charlotte, who frankly was gorgeous, so she didn't blame him at all.

Then he pulled out his phone and glanced at the screen before once again looking at the people who sat in front of the coffee shop. In person, he was even more dynamic, she thought. And she was at a distance. What would it be like to be up close and personal with him?

A sizzle went straight through her. Dang. It had been a long time since she'd felt a physical reaction like this. She rubbed her sweaty palms against her napkin.

Be cool.

He turned and walked over to the chamber, and she started trying to wave down the waitress to get her check. She was a little bit afraid that if she wasn't in her office he might just leave. She wanted to make a good impression on Zach because she needed him.

Or rather, the Soiree needed him. The only way they were going to really start generating word of mouth was with someone of his stature attached. And if he was kept waiting in the lobby of the chamber of commerce...well, that wouldn't be impressive at all.

The waitress still hadn't noticed her and for the first time in her life, Lila tossed some bills from her wallet on the table. Then she hurried across the street to the chamber offices and slammed into a solid chest.

"Sorry," she said, bracing her hand on the firm biceps and looking up into those mesmerizing blue eyes. Up close she saw that he had a firm jaw and his lips were full. She licked hers.

She'd finally run into Zach Benning.

"Well, hello there," Zach said, staring down into a pair of big brown eyes behind some of the largest horn-rimmed glasses he'd seen in a long time. The pretty brunette was tiny in his arms and smelled of summer flowers. Her hair was long and lustrous, and he felt the ends of it brush the backs of his hands as he caught her.

She had a cute little nose, but her mouth was full, making him wonder what she'd do if he kissed her. He was tempted, but the last time he'd followed his gut it hadn't worked out so well.

Zach set her on her feet and smiled. Very aware that he had to always be on. He lived his life in the spotlight and had no regrets about that, but at the same time he could never let his guard down.

"Hi. Um, I'm Lila Jones... I think you might be here to see me," she said, giving him one of the most guileless smiles he'd seen in a really long time.

He raised his eyebrows, smiling back at her. There was something so fresh and pure about her but also downright hot. Next to her the scandal that he'd left behind in Los Angeles made him feel...jaded and dirty.

"Yes, I am here to see you. Should we go somewhere and get a drink so we can talk?"

"My office?" she suggested.

Definitely not. He wanted to be seen in public. Actually, needed to. He should be lying low but didn't want to seem like he *was* lying low. And while being photographed with this sweet, wholesome-looking girl probably wouldn't hurt his reputation, it would definitely help hers.

"It's such a nice day, be a shame to spend it inside. I noticed a coffee shop across the way," he said, putting his hand on the small of her back.

"Are you sure? I noticed that blonde lady storming off when you pulled up…"

"Don't worry about her," he told her with a shrug. Tawny would be back when she cooled down. The fact was she liked the attention that being with him brought her. There were times when he wondered why they kept hooking up when they knew it would fail, but that was part of the charm. Both of them were too used to being the diva to give it up.

"Well, thank you for coming," she said, looking both ways before crossing the street, then putting her hand on his arm to keep him from walking until it was clear.

He couldn't remember the last time someone had done that. There was something so innately kind about her that it struck a chord with him. He tucked that information away because it was different from what he was accustomed to, and he wondered why he'd even noticed it.

Zach followed her and she gestured for him to sit down at the table she'd picked.

"I've been meaning to check out the Lone Star State for a while," he admitted. "My grandfather was born in Texas and used to tell me stories about growing up here."

"In Royal?" she asked curiously.

"No. Dallas. So not too far from here. You just gave me the perfect excuse to come to Texas."

She wrinkled her nose at him as if she didn't buy that. But he wasn't going to let her see any cracks in his story. If there was one thing he was good at, it was making sure everyone saw only what he wanted them to see.

"So tell me a little bit about you and your event."

"Me? There's not much to tell. I work for the Royal Chamber of Commerce, I spend my evenings reading or bingeing shows, and I have brunch with my mom and dad every weekend. What about you?"

Lila was cute and honest. She wasn't grabbing her phone and asking for a selfie or trying to pretty herself up for him. He liked that confidence she had in herself.

He felt a zing of awareness.

Why?

She wasn't his normal type. He didn't sleep with women who went home to their books and had brunch with their parents in a quiet little town. On the contrary, he was attracted to gals who knew the score. Who were used to taking what they needed and using it to get ahead. He had the feeling as much as Lila had reached out to ask him to help with this event, she wasn't a user. "Me? I'm an open book. Tell me about the Soiree." He didn't want to talk about himself; he wanted to listen to her voice instead. It was sweet and melodic.

"Well, there will be two main stages and some smaller venues for music acts. The lineup is still being put together and I can't reveal any names yet, but there are some big ones on it."

"Good. So is it a music festival?"

"Yes, but so much more. We will have three restaurants at the event."

"Where are you holding the festival? I know your text said Appaloosa Island, but I've never heard of that."

"It's in Trinity Bay, only a three-hour drive from here. We can go and check out the festival site if you'd like."

"I would. Then I'll know what we are dealing with," he said. "Is it only accessible by car and ferry?"

"We? Does that mean I can count on you?" she asked.

Count on him.

Not likely. He had to see more of this event. Right now, it sounded like some sort of small-time festival… though he knew that the Edmond family had put their weight behind the event, which should help bring in some big bucks. But it still didn't sound like the kind of thing his followers would be interested in.

"Let's see," he said. "I like to have all the facts first."

She smiled at him then. "Me, too. Everyone wants a snap decision, but it takes time to weigh all the options. To answer your other question, the island has a private landing strip and can be reached via private plane or helicopter."

She really was too adorable for words. Suddenly he felt another jolt of pure desire go through him. He wanted her. How was that even possible? While there was no doubt she was smart—he could easily read her intelligence in the questions she asked and the way she talked—she wasn't for him. They came from two different worlds and had little in common. Too bad his body didn't seem to care.

"Are you married, Lila?"

"No. Why?" she asked, appearing startled by the question.

"Boyfriend?"

She shook her head. "I don't think that is relevant."

"It is to me."

She looked as if she wanted to ask more questions, but he stopped her by standing up. "Should I drive us to Appaloosa Island?"

"No, I'll drive. I can expense the mileage. I don't want you to have to pay for the gas."

That made him laugh. He'd needed a change, which was why he'd left LA, but even he couldn't have guessed how much he'd enjoy this break.

Inviting Zach to ride in Milo might not have been her brightest idea. Watching him fold his large frame into her passenger seat would be interesting. She'd never been much for following famous Instagrammers and had maybe been a bit judgy thinking they'd be shallow—because this guy certainly wasn't.

It had almost seemed as if he were flirting with her. But no, he couldn't have been. She was nothing—*nothing*—like the blonde who had stormed away from him. In fact, the more she thought about it, the more she was sure she'd imagined the flirting.

She sighed inwardly. He did have that kissable mouth and honestly he looked better than she imagined Jane Austen's Mr. Darcy in her head. And he was the guy she always pictured when she thought of hotties. But she had to nip this ridiculous little infatuation she had for him in the bud. *Now*. Before she made a complete fool of herself.

Her convertible Mini Cooper was in good condition but a bit old. And she'd never really concerned herself with the appearance of her vehicle before she led him to it in the parking lot behind the chamber of commerce building.

She pulled her prescription sunglasses from her oversize cross-body bag and held her keys loosely in her hand. Zach had stopped walking when they'd gotten close to her car as his phone started dinging. He looked at the screen of his device and then back at her.

"Give me a minute, doll," he said. "I've got to take care of this."

"Take as long as you need. And my name is Lila, not doll," she said, smartly. She had the feeling that this was the real Zach Benning. The kind of guy who used a nickname for all women so he didn't mess up their names.

"Fair enough… I didn't mean any insult," he said. "Bad habit."

"Due to the frequency with which you change

girlfriends no doubt," she remarked. "Take care of your business. I'm going to get the air running in the car."

Though it was only May, it was Texas and they'd already had a few sweltering days. It wasn't too bad right now but her car, which had been sitting in the lot all day, would need time to cool down.

She got behind the wheel and took a few moments to put her purse on the floor behind her seat after removing two refillable water bottles that she'd put ice and water in for them both. Three hours was a long drive and she wanted Zach to get a good impression of Royal's hospitality.

"Zach Benning is in trouble again. Busted coming out of a nightclub with the wife of record exec Dom Deluca," the radio deejay said. "Apparently there was a confrontation…more to come."

Zach opened the door just as they moved on to the latest drama between two *Rich Wives* who were feuding. She looked over at him as he slid into the passenger seat and put on his seat belt. He'd had a fight with the husband of his lover. Even if he had in fact been flirting with her, there was a lot more to Zach than she wanted to invite into her life.

"I guess the married woman question makes sense now," she said.

He arched one eyebrow at her.

"Deluca."

He shook his head. "I had no idea she was married or whose wife she was."

"So you decided to start asking?"

"Yeah. Don't want any more of that kind of trouble. My old man cheated on my mom, and while I know their marriage wasn't perfect and they both had faults, that's one thing I've always tried to avoid."

"Fair enough. You moved on pretty fast with that blonde, though."

"You are fixated on Tawny, aren't you?" he asked drolly.

"You asked me some personal questions, *doll*, you've got to expect the same in return."

He almost laughed again, which made her smile. She wasn't going to let him walk all over her. That wasn't her way. She really wanted the Soiree to succeed and she was going to do everything she could to make that happen. Even flirting with Mr. Million Followers.

"Tawny isn't my girlfriend—she's sort of one of my most loyal fans. I posted in my Benningnite group that I was coming to Royal and she pinged and asked to tag along," he said.

"*Benningnite* group?" she asked as she started driving toward Trinity Bay. This man was way out of her league. He was charming and of course had that underlying sexuality that made it impossible for her not to want to stare at him. But she wasn't going to. Zach was here for business and that was it. She'd never had a problem keeping men and business separate, she didn't want to start mixing the two now.

"Yeah. I know how it sounds but some of my most loyal followers started it," he told her. "I like it."

"Okay, I think it's odd but that is your world. So, did you come here because you were interested in the festival or to avoid Deluca?" she asked. "I mean, we don't really want any negative publicity."

"What do you think he's going to do? Come to Royal and challenge me to fight?"

She shook her head. When he put it like that, she sort of felt foolish for asking, but she didn't like taking risks. He had followers which was great, and what she needed for the event, but if he was going to bring negative publicity—she'd wait and find someone else. "Make fun all you want but I have to ask these kinds of questions."

"You do? For who?" he prodded. "Is this committee worried about my personal life?"

She shrugged, a little embarrassed because she knew they weren't. The truth was, *she* wanted to know the deets. "Probably not. I mean, I don't want any trouble, but if I'm being totally honest here, it's also for myself. I usually just listen to Hollywood gossip and this is the first time I actually have met someone who is the focus of it."

"It's not as fun as you might think," he said gruffly. "But you do get used to it. So you like tea?"

She knew he meant tea as in spilling the dirt on someone famous. "I do. I hate drama in my life, but I really love listening to it in others'. Does that make me a bad person?"

"Not in my book. If you weren't interested, some of those people wouldn't have a career."

"Probably," she conceded with a laugh. "That entire world of social influence seems strange to me. I mean my parents have real jobs where they go into work and get paid. But I love the *Rich Wives* shows... those women are paid to let a camera follow them around doing outrageous stuff. It's hard to comprehend."

He laughed at that. "Yeah, I know. I am on the periphery of that. I have a lot of followers due to my lifestyle and I make money for promoting products, but I do have a real job."

He did?

"You do?"

"Yeah, having fun and giving everyone a lifestyle to aspire to."

She shook her head. "I'm not sure that's a real job, but I'm glad that you have all those followers."

"Why?"

"So they will come to the Soiree," she said. "If one of your groupies took a ride with you from LA to Texas, imagine how many will flock to our event if they know you will be there."

"So you're using me?"

"Yeah," she admitted, taking her eyes off the road to grin at him. "But I think you like that."

"We will see."

Two

They got out of her car when they got onto the ferry that would take them from Trinity Bay to Appaloosa Island. Mustang Point was an elite waterside community, and he was impressed by the yachts moored in the marina. This was his type of place. And hopefully it would distract him from Lila—the drive down had only heightened his awareness of her. He was trying to find the chink in her armor but so far, he hadn't. To be honest, he wasn't looking that hard.

She paid for their tickets and chatted with the man who was selling them. If Zach had learned anything on the three-hour drive, it was that Lila was open and friendly. There was something almost innocent about her and it was refreshing after the LA scene, where everyone was trying to outshine one another.

Lila walked back over to him, her wide-leg pants undulating with each step. His eyes drifted upward to assess the rest of her outfit. She had on a slim-fitting Breton shirt, which showed off her slender waist and the curve of her breasts. Again, he wondered why she was single. He wasn't going to make the mistake of asking her another pointed question... or was he? She intrigued him.

True, he was bored and at loose ends while he figured out his next move, but still he tried to reassure himself that he would have found her interesting even if he wasn't in this rather small Texas town. He knew that was a lie and while he had no problem putting on a facade for his followers, he had always tried to never lie to himself.

That was a path that he had long ago realized if he started down, he'd never come back from. His life was all about showing off; he knew that it was smoke and mirrors, and most of the time that didn't bother him. *Oh, hell.* Was he getting melancholy? He shook his head. It was just being here in the state his grandfather had talked so much about, stirring up old dreams that were better left in the past. And of course, Lila stirring up new desires that he knew had no future.

"The ferry will be leaving in ten minutes," she told him. "There aren't a lot of facilities on the island so if you need...well, it's over there."

She sort of blushed when she gestured and he turned to see what she was pointing to.

The ferry offices were there, and he noticed a restroom sign. He almost laughed again. She was too much. Just so *different*. He liked it. A little too much, he thought. He was in Texas to lie low, not start something with this small-town sweetheart.

"I'm fine," he said.

"Okay. So, um, now that I'm not concentrating on driving, do you have any questions for me?"

He did. But he knew she wasn't inviting him to probe into her personal life. He was also curious about how she'd feel in his arms and what her kiss would be like. Prim and proper...or hot and unrestrained? She was a mix of both things and he wondered if there was something in her past that made her hide that side of herself. "I'll wait until I've seen the facilities. The pdf you supplied was interesting." A bit dull. But perhaps that was only because of the document. He wanted to see the venues before he made any judgments.

"That's fair. I haven't been out here since all of the construction has been completed. I'm really impressed by the committee so far. I don't want to let them down," she said.

"You won't."

"I wish I had your confidence...and your followers," she confessed.

His *followers*.

He seemed to have an instinct for posting the

right sort of photos and wording his text in a way that people liked. A lot of the time, especially in the beginning, he'd been sarcastic, and his audience had thought he was joking. They loved his sense of humor. Which in a way had given him carte blanche to be himself. Or this version of himself. Speaking of which, he hadn't posted for almost twenty-four hours on his social media channels. He'd needed time to think. To regroup and figure out his next move. He enjoyed his bad-boy reputation, but he had always felt that he was a good man…until now.

He wondered if he'd become too inured in his lifestyle and lost a part of himself. Sleeping with a married woman—that was a line too far. And Ms. Jones was the balm for that.

His mom had texted him as he'd left LA…one of her little nudges. She always couched it as "hope you are okay," but he knew she wanted him to get a real job. To stop making money off influencing people. So he'd just texted back a smiley face and left it at that.

"Followers are good, but if I burn them by recommending something that's not up to the normal standards, they will turn on me. And rightly so. They've put their trust in my platform and I have to make sure that I deliver."

"What exactly do you deliver?" she asked. The ferry pulled in and she walked back over to the Mini Cooper.

He followed her and got in, thinking about her

question. What *did* he deliver? "A lifestyle that is fun, sexy and luxurious. I give them something to dream about and an escape from their everyday lives."

Lila nodded as she carefully drove onto the ferry. "That's perfect for our event. I hope you will agree to share it with your followers."

She pushed her sunglasses to the top of her head, and he couldn't help noticing her pretty brown eyes. They were big and wide and she smiled easily at him. That mouth of hers tempted him, too. The full lower lip seemed to beckon him closer, but then he noticed it moving.

She was telling him something. Probably something important. Probably nothing to do with where his mind was heading.

"I'm sorry…what did you say?"

"Just that I don't think you are going to be disappointed."

Oh, hell.

He knew he wasn't going to be disappointed in the woman, but the event had *snoozefest* written all over it from what he'd read. Now he was in a quandary. Did he stay here and help her out in the hopes of getting into her pants? Or was he going to be honest and go back to LA where an angry husband was waiting for him?

No choice really.

He was going to have to find a way to make this

work, because he wasn't ready to leave Lila Jones. Not yet.

"Oh, I'm sure you and I can come up with something to keep that from happening," he said.

She blushed and nodded. "I'll do whatever I have to in order to make this event a success."

"Perfect."

Lila found Zach charming and easygoing. After the drive down she'd stopped feeling nervous about being around a man who was so famous. Well, mostly. It was hard because as she drove them off the private ferry toward the eastern side of the island, she saw people watching the car. Even when she'd been buying the ferry tickets, people had noticed him.

Mostly younger people. The young, well-heeled moneyed crowd were exactly who they wanted to attract to Soiree on the Bay. They had the energy to share on social media the charities that the committee was promoting.

"The western half of the island is famous for its pristine beaches and a small boutique hotel. There are a few large vacation homes as well," she explained. "After we see the venue, I can drive you by them if you'd like."

"Sure."

She drove away from the ferry toward the festival grounds. There hadn't been a lot on the island before they'd started constructing them. She parked in the dirt lot and put her keys in her pocket as she got out, slinging her bag over her shoulder as she waited for Zach to join her.

"This is the parking area, obviously, and that field over there beyond will be for overnighters. I'm talking to a company that does glamping pods right now."

"Glamping?"

"Yes. Well, not everyone who attends will be able to stay on their yachts, and the community of Mustang Point only has 750 hotel rooms. And the boutique hotel is very small. They do have a golf cart and Jeep service to pick up guests and bring them from the landing strip or this side of the island back to the resort."

"Um-hmm," he said.

She wasn't sure how to respond to that, so she put on her best tour guide voice and smile and led him around the island. "This is the second music venue, sort of the smaller stage. I was thinking, like Glastonbury, it will be a place for up-and-coming artists to showcase their talent."

"That's a good idea. Have you talked to any record companies?"

"I have some feelers out," she said. Not wanting to let him know that once he was on board and they started generating some real promotional buzz, she would make the calls. She didn't want their top choices to turn the Soiree down before she had done this kind of work.

"Over here will be the first of the three restaurants. It's sort of based on a sports bar with a fusion menu. It will be open 24/7, serving both in the restaurant and some takeaway basket–type prepared meals."

"Do you have a celebrity chef doing the menus?"

"I'm not sure. I think so. I can find out and let you know. I know that another member of the planning committee is handling that."

He nodded again. Then waited for her to go on.

Lila wasn't sure what he was thinking. She kept getting distracted by the spicy scent of his aftershave and the way that the sun brought out the highlights in his thick brown hair. The breeze on the island swirled around them, ruffling his hair, but it always landed back in the perfect spot. Her own mane, on the other hand, felt like it was growing with the humidity. And she was pretty sure that it was getting frizzy despite the products she'd put in it earlier in the day.

She showed him the rest of the venue and he asked a few questions but not really that many. Tension gnawed at her. She was worried that he wasn't impressed, and she had no idea how to wow him. But she was determined to do whatever she had to in order to get him on board with the event.

"How do you feel about grabbing a drink at the hotel?" she asked. "We can discuss your thoughts there."

"Sounds great," he said.

She drove them over there, and they were seated on the patio of the restaurant, which afforded them an unspoiled view of the bay. He ordered a Jack and Coke. She had sparkling water with a twist of lime.

Finally she couldn't wait any longer. "So what do you think? Will you let your followers know about the Soiree on the Bay?"

He took a sip of his drink, then leaned back. "There are a lot of festivals out there. Why should people come to yours?"

Well, he had her there. Why *should* they? They weren't Coachella, but she felt with the right planning and people in place they could be. "I don't know. I'm not sure I can figure that out on my own."

"Don't worry, I can. What you need is sizzle."

Sizzle.

"I mean I can guarantee some sizzle from the Texas heat, and the food is going to be great, but I'm sure that's not what you meant."

"It isn't."

She knew it. She looked into Zach's blue eyes. He had sizzle. Oodles of it. And sex appeal. But there was no way she could figure out how to get that into the event. Not on her own. She'd tried to do sexy one time and it had backfired—big-time. Convincing her to stick to what she knew. Who she was. And she was that quirky, smart girl whom everyone liked. Not a hot fantasy woman.

"So what should we do? I mean you are absolutely right. We don't have anything that makes us stand out."

"Don't worry, Lila, I got this."

"You got this?" she asked. "Sure, you have your own brand of sizzle but I don't see how that's going to translate to Soiree on the Bay."

"You think I have that?" he asked, leaning in, and she noticed the tiny gray flecks in his irises. He smiled at her and wriggled his eyebrows.

He liked to flirt, and she had to admit she wasn't used to that sort of attention from any guy. She was the reliable woman everyone turned to in order to get things done. But Zach acted like…well, like she was that hot blonde who'd stalked away from his car. Okay, that might be an exaggeration, but he seemed to actually see her. And that was new. She kind of liked it but at the same time, she was scared. No one had ever really seen through her quirkiness. She knew she used it as a shield. And now she was wondering what she was going to do with Zach.

"You know you do," Lila said, taking a sip of her sparkling water. She'd put on those thick-rimmed sunglasses of hers so he couldn't see her eyes. Only himself reflected in the lenses. He looked good in this light, but he wanted to know more about *her*.

"You're right, I definitely do," he admitted. His mom had always said that he was born with the spotlight on him. He just had naturally gravitated to attention. And yeah, he liked it and had luckily found a way to cultivate that into the life he wanted.

"So humble."

"Listen, why pretend that I can't see what I'm

good at?" he asked, grinning at her. He wasn't like Lila—he didn't want to blend into the background. And to be honest, he wondered if she wanted that for herself. Though she was a plain dresser, her attitude and her personality were anything but. Lila Jones was born to sparkle, but for some reason she hid that side of herself. He wanted to know why.

She just smiled and shook her head. "Why indeed. Actually, that is why I contacted you. If you promoted our event. Just talked about it…"

He could. But he wasn't sure that he was going to be able to spend the kind of time in Texas that he needed to in order to help her that way. It would be better if she had a following that she could use to promote her cause.

"What's your social media account?" he asked.

"What? Um…I messaged you from it. LilaJones93."

He pulled it up and there were a grand total of twelve pictures listed on the account. The most recent had been last Christmas and a photo of her tea in a Christmas mug that said I've Been Good. The account seemed like it would belong to, well, a grandma and not the young hip kind, but one who was ninety-three. "No offense, but your account screams crazy cat lady."

"Okay. Calm down. Not everyone is so obsessed with themselves that they feel they need to post a selfie four times a day."

"It's six, actually," he said. "And you reached out to me. So I'm guessing you wanted feedback."

"Feedback on the event. Not a personal critique of my own social media presence. Or lack thereof. But that is my life. I have my job and my quiet life. I know it's not going to bring the 'sizzle' you're talking about. But I'm not you."

No, she wasn't him. But she could be with a few tweaks. He shouldn't have been so blunt in his assessment of her Instagram account and he knew she'd taken it as an attack on her way of life. Which was as foreign to him as his was to her. But as she'd so aptly pointed out, it was *her* life.

"I'm sorry for what I said," he apologized. "I never meant to hurt your feelings."

"It's okay. I'm glad you were honest with me," she admitted. "It's just who I am."

This was who she was? No way. Lila was so much more than a few pictures of teacups and books or the PBS Masterpiece screenshots she posted. She was funny, witty, smart and someone people would find engaging…if she changed a few things.

And she was the perfect distraction, he thought. No use trying to pretend he wasn't doing this for himself. He wanted her, but the way she was right now…well, there was a very real chance he'd hurt her if they had a summer hookup. But if he helped her out of her shell, showed her how to be that sassy woman she kept hidden behind her plain clothing and thick glasses, maybe a few nights burning up the sheets with him would be enough. And maybe, along the way, he'd start feeling like himself again.

"I have an idea," he said. The thought had come to him suddenly. He knew how to make anyone famous in the social media world and then translate that to the real world. He'd done it for many of his protégés. And he could do it for her.

"Great. That's why I asked you here."

That smart mouth just made him want to kiss her. But he wasn't going to. Not yet, anyway. Zach wanted to prove his point that she was hiding her true self behind her girl-next-door persona. He knew she believed in herself, so why was she shy at times and feisty at others? His eyes roved over her, drinking in every gorgeous facet. He wanted to pull that dynamic woman to the surface. Show her the sizzle she had deep inside and for some reason was afraid to show the world.

"What if I told you that I could make you famous? That you could promote the Soiree on the Bay without me."

"I'd say the Texas sun has gotten to you," she said, laughing. "I promise you right now that won't happen."

"If you put yourself in my hands it will," he assured her. "In fact, I bet you right now that if we go into the shop in the lobby and get you a different outfit, I could post a picture of you that will get over five hundred likes in the first hour."

"And if it doesn't?" she asked. "Will you give up this notion and promote the event from your own account? And attend all of the press events?"

He narrowed his eyes. She was fighting this change. He got it. For as much as he put himself out there every day, there were still pockets of truth he hid from the world. Was he urging her to do this for any reason other than as a sop for his conscience so he could feel okay about seducing her?

He turned away from her. Forced himself to be real for a minute. As much as he wanted Lila in his arms, he wanted the world to see that beautiful, quirky, sassy woman.

He saw what she was doing but he knew that under his guidance he could create a social media image for Lila Jones that would garner more attention than she ever dreamed possible. "You have to do exactly what I say. That means clothes, hair, *everything*…and I'll tell you what to post until you get the hang of it. No quibbles."

"No quibbles? Exactly what does that mean?" she asked.

"That I get final approval on everything you wear and eat and talk about on your account. I get to mold you."

"Mold me? I like me."

"I like you, too, Lila. But no one is noticing you the way you are now. I'm not talking about changing you, I'm talking about dressing you and photographing you in a way that shows the world the real Lila. That way the success of the event is yours." This was his hard sell. She hadn't come to him asking to be Insta-famous, and if he was honest, a part of him expected her to turn him down. But another part, that deep-seated masculine part, sensed she'd rise to the challenge. His gut told him there was a part of her that wanted to stop blending in with the background.

"I don't need the success to be mine," she said. "The committee has a lot of really talented people on it."

"Including you." She was too quick to hide her own sparkle and he didn't understand what made her do it.

But regardless, he wanted to change that. Of course he knew once she started getting the attention she'd change. Maybe lose a little of that innocence, and then he wouldn't feel so bad about flirting with her and maybe getting her in his bed. Then they'd be a part of the same world and understand that nothing lasted.

He felt a pang.

Did he want to do that?

She was more complicated than he wanted her to be. But then so was life. And it was her decision. "So what'll it be? You in?"

She didn't answer immediately and he wondered if she would turn him down. He was asking her to change a lot about herself and he could tell she wasn't unhappy with her life.

He wanted to get back to that himself.

"Okay, doll, you've got yourself a deal."

Three

Lila felt foolish as she stood in the dressing area of the chic boutique in the island resort. Zach had nudged her toward the changing area, asked the shop attendant to get her a glass of champagne and told her to wait.

She'd declined the champagne. That wasn't her style, but she went and sat down. Everything in this shop was totally out of her budget. She hoped that they would be amenable to some sort of payment plan where she put the pieces on different credit cards. Ugh. Why had she agreed to do this?

Truth be told, she had never really been that interested in fashion. She liked her clothes comfortable, and she kept her hair trimmed and occasionally wore lipstick, but that was it. That one time she'd tried to be different—no. She wasn't going there. She liked herself just as she was. This makeover was all about Zach. Because she needed him to help promote the Soiree, and if this was what she had to do to get him on board, then so be it.

Bottom line? They had gotten a lot of charities involved and they wanted to get A-list stars and chefs at the event, so she needed to do this. She wanted the event to be successful. Also, she was honest enough to admit that she liked Zach. His challenge was silly but the thought of having his full, undivided attention was…*intoxicating*.

"Where's the champagne?" he asked when he came into the dressing area with another shop assistant she hadn't seen earlier following him with a wheeled clothing rack.

"I decided water would be fine. Who's that?"

"This is Georgia. She's one of the Benningnites. She spotted us when we were having our drinks and volunteered to help out."

"It's no problem at all, ZB. I'm so thrilled to do it! Who is this?" Georgia asked, pointing at her.

"This is the woman I am making over," he said. "She and I have a little bet that I can't get her five hundred likes in an hour."

Georgia raised her eyebrows as if "ZB" had bitten off more than he could chew. Lila bit the inside of her cheek to keep from smiling. "I don't know if these clothes are going to be enough to do that."

"Trust me," Zach said. "Georgia, will you go and see if we can get some champagne?"

"Love to, ZB. Back in a mo," she said, turning and dashing away.

"Now, let's see," Zach said, turning back to the rack. He pulled off a pair of tiny tropical-printed shorts and a lacy top and handed them to her.

"Uh, I'm not letting you photograph me in something this…small."

"This is just so I can get an idea of your shape. Those pants and that shirt don't really tell me enough," he said. "Also, I'm offended you think I would pick something that wouldn't flatter you."

She wondered if he were pushing to see how commited she was to this makeover. She didn't blame him for picking something that was so totally different from what she was wearing.

She shook her head and took the clothing from him, going into the changing room without saying another word. He'd asked her for her sizes, so she knew they'd fit. She'd been a solid size 10 since eighth grade and rarely fluctuated. She knew it was trendy to be 00 but Lila liked food and not worrying about her figure too much to try to fit into that size. Her mom had once joked that the Jones women had hips; no use trying to pretend they didn't.

She took off her shoulder bag and placed it on one of the hooks on the wall. Then turned back and looked at herself in the mirror. Was she going to do this? She felt like she could back out at any time, but she knew if she did Zach was out the door.

Lila stopped debating and got changed. The shorts were shorter than she normally would wear but they were cute and the top…it was flattering, too, revealing her arms and scooping down over her breasts.

What would Zach think when he saw her? Oh, gosh, what if he didn't see any difference? Or if he was like—*no*. She couldn't let her mind go there. The clothes didn't change who she was at her core.

She forced herself to open the changing-room door and stepped out find Zach nowhere around. But she could hear his voice in the other room, and he was laughing and joking with someone. She went to peek out and see who he was talking to. A group of men and women were smiling at him and snapping selfies.

Oh, for Pete's sake.

At this rate, she was going to be here all day waiting for him.

"Hey, ZB, if you can spare a minute, I'm ready," she called to him.

"Later," Zach said to his fans, and came back over to her.

He took her hand in his, pulling her arm away from her body as his gaze scrutinized her from head to toe. She felt a tingle as if he were touching her as his eyes moved over her neck, lingering on the curve of her breasts, before he finished looking down her body.

She shifted her legs as his gaze lasered in on them. She pulled her hand back and put it around her waist. This was a mistake.

Of course she never could resist a dare, and this had felt like one. But standing here, feeling so vulnerable...

She hated this.

"Nice legs, Lila," he said. His voice was deeper, huskier. "You look fabulous. I really like this on you. Do you?"

She scrunched up her mouth. His words washed away some of the self-consciousness that had settled on her. She turned back to the full-length mirror and saw herself this time without the fear and doubt. If she was doing this, she needed to be honest. Both with him and herself. "Yes, but not for a photo. I'd prefer to have my legs covered to mid-thigh, and the top is light and airy but the scoop is lower than I like."

"Okay. I can work with that," he said. "Now what about shoes?"

"These are fine," she said. "Already I'm going to be paying off these clothes for a few months."

"Oh, this is all on me," he said. "Then if you are as popular as I think you will be, the rest of your wardrobe will be gratis."

Gratis.

Who did he think he was? She wasn't going to argue with him just now. "Wardrobe?"

"Yes. If this works, one photo won't be enough.

You're going to have to keep posting. Every day, Lila, not just at Christmas."

She laughed at him, tossing her hair, and for the first time she really let her guard down with him. There was something about Zach that felt very open and real, as if he were just what she saw. Though she knew everyone had hidden layers. "If it works. If not, then you will be posting about the Soiree."

"If this makeover fails...then yeah, I will fulfill my end of the deal. But I'm sure it won't. Now give me a minute to think about what will look best on you. Can you wear a heel?"

"Yes, I like the added height."

"I thought so. I noticed those chunky Mary Janes you were wearing."

"They are comfortable. Shoes have to be."

"Agreed."

She waited while he went over the rack of clothing and then put several things in the dressing room. Georgia came back with a waiter from the bar and a standing ice bucket with a bottle of champagne in it and three glasses. Lila left them to their drinks and went into the changing room to try on the clothes he'd put in there. She shook her head. The colors were bold and eye-catching. Not her normal muted navy, peach and cream.

"Come out when you have the first outfit on. Wear everything I provided, and oh, here are some shoes."

He pushed a pair of strappy gold sandals under the door.

What had she gotten herself into?

* * *

Zach waited for Lila to change, trying to forget how hot she'd looked in those shorts. He had suspected she had a killer body under those sensible clothes, but he hadn't anticipated how turned on he'd get just from seeing her in clothing that fit her.

The sooner he got Lila out of her shell the better. Though he wondered if she was going to really let herself be comfortable in anything he chose. Speaking of which…she was taking a lot longer in the dressing room than he'd expected.

It had been funny to him that she hadn't believed him when he'd said she'd be popular. He knew the way followers reacted online and he was steering Lila to the sort of persona that would have the maximum effect. Also, his gut was seldom wrong.

Once she was popular, once she was like all the other women he knew, then…well then, he'd know how to handle her. He'd feel comfortable just being his flawed self around her. Instead of the guilt mixed with lust he felt right now.

Zach glanced toward the dressing room again. He wasn't nervous, but he was anxiously waiting to see her in the clothes he'd selected.

He'd settled on a classic A-line dress with a halter neckline. It was universally flattering and had a timelessness to the look, which he suspected Lila would appreciate. Georgia was chattering on about her summer and how she felt so lucky she was on Appaloosa Island when he'd arrived.

"Why are you here?" Georgia asked.

"I heard there was going to be a luxury food, art and wine festival here and wanted to check it out," he said.

"Are you coming back for it? I've heard about it, too, but I thought it was going to just be another event in the Mustang Point social calendar."

"It's going to be big," he stated, with a certain vagueness. He wasn't willing to commit to attending the event yet. There were still too many unknowns. Like if it would be a success or not. He wouldn't endorse something that might fail.

"I'll tell all my friends," she promised.

Her phone chimed and she groaned. "I have to go. Will you be here for a while?"

"Heading out in a short while. But it was great to see you," he said. "Maybe I'll see you at the Soiree."

She smiled and waved as she left. He took another sip of the champagne and waited. Scrolling through his social media feeds, he noticed that he'd been tagged in a lot of photos this afternoon. Well, he wasn't off the radar. Which was fine.

Zach grimaced when he saw a DM from the husband of the woman he'd been caught with. He wasn't about to open *that*. Instead, he delegated it to his assistant. That was why Dawn worked for him.

He heard the door of the dressing room open and glanced up and nearly lost his breath. The transformation wasn't complete, but in clothing that actually fit her and with those heels on…Lila Jones was a knockout.

He was trying to make it physical but when their eyes met and she smiled at him, he felt something… something he'd never felt before. But he refused to let this be anything other than fun and flirty. That was it. All he had to give to anyone.

A therapist he'd seen after his parents' divorce had pointed out that he was reluctant to create any lasting bonds and Zach had shrugged it off. But those words lingered in his mind and he felt more and more that he'd never be able to be anything more than the photos on his feed.

And damn, she was hot. He had sensed it when he'd seen her in the shorts and scoop-neck blouse but this was next level. The confidence she'd always had was suddenly front and center. She wasn't trying to wrap her arms around herself like she had earlier.

He had included a headband and some various hair accessories that he'd seen in the shop, and he was pleased to see that she had pulled her hair up into a high ponytail, which left her shoulders bare. She'd even put on the earrings he'd selected.

He stood up, putting his champagne glass down before he walked over to her. God. How was he going to hide his reaction? Did he *have* to? "Damn, I'm good."

"*You're* good? I'm the one wearing it."

"And you wear it well," he rasped. "Step up here."

He gestured to the step situated in front of the three-mirror setup. Offering her his hand as she

stepped up there. The mirror gave him every angle of
her outfit and honestly there wasn't a bad one. Well,
except for those rather large glasses, but they were
cute and Lila. IRL—in real life—they'd be okay, but
not for the photo he had in mind.

"Wait here."

He turned and went back into the main store area
and sorted through the designer sunglasses on the
rack. Finally settling on a pair of black cat's-eye
frames. They weren't too big and would be perfect on
her heart-shaped face. He brought them back in and
stood next to her on the step in front of the mirror.

"Turn toward me," he commanded.

She did and he reached for her glasses, taking
them off. She blinked at him as he did so. For this
one moment when she couldn't see he let his guard
down. Looked at her with the hunger she'd stirred
deep inside him.

"What are you doing?" she asked. "These aren't
for show. I need them to see."

"Trust me," he said. He needed her trust…needed
her to follow wherever he led. And he honestly didn't
want to go much farther than back in that dressing room so he could kiss her until they were both
breathless and naked.

"You ask that a lot, don't you?"

"Just of you. Most people inherently do," he said.

"Most people are waiting to be told what to do,"
she retorted.

"Not you," he said, reaching up and pulling a few

tendrils out of her ponytail to frame her face and then decided that they were too much and tucked them back behind her ear. He was trying to make her look like other influencers he knew but even in the same outfit she was still Lila Jones. Still so different from them. It wasn't the clothes, it was the woman.

Then he put the sunglasses on and stepped back. "Perfect."

"If I could see myself, I'd let you know if I agreed."

He almost laughed at the way she said it. "Put your glasses on and then step down and we'll find a good place to photograph you."

"Sure."

She took her glasses from him and a tingle went up his arm as their hands touched. He wanted to pretend it was just static electricity. But he knew it was more. He wanted her. He'd wanted her before when she'd been sweet and shy little Lila, but with the fashionable new clothes and hair…she was making him hard and addling his senses.

He was thinking that he wished he'd brought his private jet instead of his Ferrari to Texas, because then he could have swept Lila onto it and taken her someplace exotic and intimate.

"Zach…?"

"I'm sorry, what did you say?"

"I asked if I should leave my clothes in the changing room?"

"Yes. We are coming back."

She dashed in and grabbed that hideous bag of hers and he shook his head. "Not that sack."

She almost hugged the purse to her chest. "What's wrong with it?"

"Too much to explain. We will find something suitable before we leave. Let's go take a photo and see if this works."

"Oh, okay. But I'm not giving up my purse."

Zach didn't argue with her. Instead, he told the shop assistant they'd be back in a few minutes and led Lila out into the lobby, where he found the right background for the photo. He took her hideous bag and put it by his feet and then took her glasses and made her put on the sunglasses he'd found.

"I don't know why I'm wearing sunglasses inside," she complained.

"And that's why you have so few people following you on social media." As he moved back to take the picture, he noticed that the men and women in the lobby were watching them. He heard someone ask who the woman was and smiled to himself.

This bet was in the bag. But he knew that this was never about winning, it was about getting Lila into his bed. About making her into the kind of woman that he could hook up with and not have regrets. He felt that twinge again deep inside. Why was he trying to take someone who had been unique, beautiful and natural and make her into a woman like so many others?

Because he was selfish and wanted her more than he should.

* * *

Lila felt silly posing in the lobby of the chic boutique resort on Trinity Bay. It was odd, but when she'd been alone with Zach, she hadn't felt silly. As soon as she filtered out the other people and just concentrated on him, her nerves settled. Of course, once he'd taken her glasses from her and insisted she put on the sunglasses, she couldn't really see anything but blurry images.

That was oddly freeing.

She didn't worry about what anyone else was thinking about what she was doing because she couldn't see them. All she could truly concentrate on was Zach's voice. He told her how to stand and how to pose and when to smile, and she did it.

He took—no lie—about a million pictures. Or at least it felt that way to her. She wondered if he really thought that he was going to be able to make her into a social media star with just a change of outfit.

But she knew he didn't. He'd said *wardrobe*. Yet while he wanted this change to be permanent, she wasn't sure she did. He finally stopped and came back over to her.

"We are done for now," he said. "Here are your glasses. What do you think?"

He handed her his phone and at first she barely recognized herself. She'd felt sort of different when she'd seen herself in the mirror, but not being able to see everyone else in the lobby had been more liberating than she'd imagined. There was a playfulness and a confidence to her poses that she'd never seen in herself before.

"I like them."

It made her wonder why she hadn't thought to try this before. But she wasn't interested in delving into her psyche at the moment. "What now?"

"Well, I'm going to reach out to Warby Parker after we get your photo trending and ask them to make you some new glasses and sunglasses," he said. "But first let's pay for these clothes and then I'll show you how to post your picture to get the maximum likes."

Lila doubted that Warby Parker was going to want her wearing their glasses, and as much as the photo made her feel different, she still wasn't sure that Zach's confidence wasn't misplaced. She followed him back across the lobby and noticed that people were watching them. Of course they were. She was with Mr. Über Famous who just took it all in stride. But the eyes on her…well, it was flattering, but she was used to a certain amount of anonymity.

Zach had her old clothes wrapped up and put in a bag, which the shop attendant handed to her with a smile. "You look great."

"Thanks."

He led her back outside until they were standing with the bay to their back. "Put your sunglasses on."

She did it and he put his arm around her waist and pulled her close.

"What are you doing?" she asked. Trying to ignore the fact that her heart was beating faster and that she could feel the heat of his hand through her dress on her waist.

"Taking a selfie. We are about to start your social media climb," he said.

He put his sunglasses on, stretched his arm out and snapped a picture of the two of them.

"So never post a photo without editing it. Every platform has its own size that works best. I'll Air-Drop you the dimensions when we are done. Next you want to find a filter that works best for you. I'd try this one…it's my favorite."

She leaned in closer, resting her hand on his upper arm so she could keep see the screen. A little tingle went straight up her arm and her nipples tightened. She wasn't going to pretend she didn't want Zach.

But she was his project…

"Then when you are satisfied with the image, you need to think of the right caption. What do you think we should say?"

"This is on your account?"

"Yes, I'm going to tag you," he said. "Tell the Benningnites to follow you."

"Fun day out with @lilajones93," she suggested.

"Maybe. How about this?" he asked.

She saw he captioned their photo with, "@lila jones93 is bringing the sizzle this summer in Texas. #SoireeontheBay."

"Now what?"

"Now we wait for the likes to come flooding in.

One of my followers suggested a great seafood restaurant in Mustang Point. I'll treat you to dinner before we drive back to Royal."

Dinner?

She didn't have any plans tonight, but wasn't sure she liked that he thought she didn't. "I might have plans."

"Do you? I'm hungry. I just thought eating would be nice before we went on a three-hour drive."

Now she felt silly for even saying anything. "I was just being defensive. I hate when anyone assumes I don't have plans."

"Me, too. Do you want to eat with me?"

"I do," she admitted.

"Is seafood okay or do you have allergies?" he asked.

"Not allergic to anything but BS," she said.

"Good to know we have the same allergies," he deadpanned. "Let's get out of here."

"I'm going to have to put my prescription sunglasses on to drive," she told him.

"I'll allow it, since I'm not sure we want to be in a car accident."

"So glad you'll *allow* it… I'm a grown-ass woman, ZB," she said. "I make my own decisions."

"Oh, I know you are, LJ. I was teasing."

"Fair enough. But you've been very bossy today," she reminded him.

"It was to help out Soiree on the Bay."

She nodded and didn't say anything else but

couldn't help wishing that he'd helped her out for herself and not the event. That made her face the fact that she might have agreed to the makeover because it had brought her into Zach's spotlight and she liked it more than she wanted to admit.

Four

Lila valet-parked the car and then followed Zach into the Republic of Texas Steak and Seafood House. He smiled at the maître d' and did his charming Zach thing while she hung back watching him. She wasn't sure how she felt about the afternoon. So much had changed in so little time.

Honestly, it rattled her. Probably because she didn't hate it as much as she thought she should. She had the feeling if she'd been dressed like this, Zach would have noticed her when he'd pulled up.

Her phone pinged and she saw it was a text from her mom.

Honey, you look great in that picture. Are you dating that guy?

Thanks, Mom. He's a work friend. For Soiree on the Bay.

Try to make him a friend friend. He's cute. ;)

Mooooom.

[kissing emoji] Have fun. Text me tomorrow. We can meet for lunch or coffee. Love you.

I will. Love you, too.

"Phone blowing up with likes?" Zach asked as he came back over to her.

"Uh, no. That was my mom."

"What did she say?" he asked. "Did she approve of your look?"

She rolled her eyes. "She liked it. Said you were cute."

"I like her already." Zach grinned. "You should be getting some notifications from the post…let me see your phone."

"Why?"

"I want to make sure your notifications are turned on," he said.

"Is that important?"

He looked at her as if she'd started speaking a different language. "It's *massive*. When we are seated, I'll show you. I've already gotten a ton of likes. So I'm sure you've gotten a few."

The maître d' offered them a glass of champagne

while they were waiting to be seated and Lila almost groaned. "I have to drive home."

"What if you didn't?" Zach asked.

"Then I'd love a glass. It kind of feels like a champagne kind of day," she said. And in all honesty, Zach bought the good stuff, not the bottom-shelf grocery store sparkling wine that Lila usually purchased. "But I don't think you are going to skip drinking."

"I'm not," he said, winking at her. "Leave the details to me. We will get home safely and your car will be in your driveway in the morning."

"How?"

"Leave it to me," he repeated. "Can you do that, Lila Jones? Just stop worrying and planning and let go for one night?"

"Of course I can. I just might not want to," she huffed. But she *did* want to. She caught a glimpse of herself in the mirrored panels behind the maître d' stand. This was new Lila. "Fine. But my car better be there in the morning. I have a meeting at ten."

He just shook his head and laughed, turning to the waiter. "We'll have a bottle of champagne. Two glasses here, the rest at the table."

"Of course, sir," the waiter said, turning away.

Zach led her to a padded velvet bench and sat down next to her. "So, if you go in your app and hit the settings button you can turn on notifications."

He showed her on his phone, and she was surprised to see she already had way over five hundred likes on the photo that Zach had tagged her in. She turned on the notifications like he demonstrated and then went back to her profile to notice that her actual followers were increasing, too. By a lot.

"Uh, what's going on?" she asked Zach, showing him the increasing likes.

"You're going viral, LJ. Prepare to be famous," he said. "I need to make a quick call. I'll be back and then we will celebrate."

He got up and she stared at her phone. She couldn't believe one photo could change her online presence that much, but it had. A thrill shot through her. Zach was going to do wonders for the Soiree on the Bay. This was what the event needed. The kind of publicity that was in essence free.

Well, not really. Because no matter what he said, she'd have to pay him back for this outfit. And in regard to her "wardrobe"…she'd have to do some secondhand shopping and see what she could find. She'd never admit it to Zach, but she liked the new clothing he'd selected and she might even spring for new glasses. After all, she'd had this pair for almost five years now. Thankfully her vision had finally stopped worsening so she didn't need a new prescription, but maybe something a little trendier would be nice. Or even contacts… She could take the extra ten minutes in the morning to put them in.

"Oh, you're Lila Jones, right?"

She glanced up to see a group of three college-aged women standing there. "I am."

"We saw you with ZB. That's fab! What's this

event he was talking about? Where can we buy tickets?" one of them asked.

Lila stood up and reached into her large bag to pull out the flyers she'd made up for the event. But as she started to, Zach returned and put his hand over hers. Stopping her, and she realized why. Those flyers looked like they were made in the office. They weren't slick or professional-looking.

"Ladies, hello. Lila has a website that you can check out. Soireeonthebay.com. She's still working on the print promotion."

When he winked over at her, she felt a connection. Like they were a couple. She liked it, but she cautioned herself that it wasn't real. Zach was a man used to lots of attention and he immediately made everyone feel at ease. She was nothing special.

"Great, ZB. Can we get a selfie with you both?" one of them asked.

What was going on? This was nuts. She found it hard to believe these women wanted a picture with her. Earlier today she'd had trouble flagging down the waitress for her check…and now *this*?

"Of course," Zach said, pulling her into his side and looking down at her with an impish grin. She felt a connection with him. As much as they were in this group, they were also just the two of them. Sharing a smile over the way these women were behaving around them. He told the girls to come around behind them, then took the phone and snapped a photo.

Their waiter came back and let them know their

table was ready. *Thank goodness*. She wasn't sure she was ready for the amount of attention being with Zach garnered. He loved it, she noticed, but he didn't shove her to the side. He included her, which she liked. He seemed to want to share the spotlight with her.

"See you at the Soiree," he murmured, putting his hand on the small of her back as they followed the waiter.

She felt an electric tingle go down her spine and she realized how long it had been since her last date. This was business, but she couldn't help herself. She liked Zach and a part of her wanted this to be personal. Though that was crazy, because his life was on a different level than hers. And changing her clothing and her look was one thing. She wasn't interested in changing her life.

They'd been seated at the best table in the house next to a large glass window that provided spectacular water views. As the sun set, the lights from the marina reflected on the bay, the yachts that were moored in the water came to life, and for once, Zach didn't feel that gnawing need to be somewhere else. He'd always had something worse than FOMO—fear of missing out—and had always struggled to be content with what he had and where he was.

But with Lila sitting across from him, gazing alternately at her phone, which kept lighting up with notifications, and then out the window at the bay, it felt different. She *enchanted* him. He knew it was because she was new. It had happened before. He also knew he was going to just go for it. Follow this feeling for as long and as far as he could.

In a way, dating one girl had always stirred that feeling of missing out, like there was another woman that he'd have more fun with. One woman couldn't tame him. He loved women, but he had never been satisfied by just one. For now, though, Lila was enough.

"What are you thinking?" he asked. "You keep staring at the yachts."

"Just wondering where they have been... Actually, that's not true. I'm staring out there because when I look at my phone, I can't believe that people liked our photo that much and then I panic thinking how am I going to sustain that kind of thing. Is it a fluke?"

Zach couldn't remember a time when he worried about anything like that. He'd been famous since he was in his early twenties...and knew that he was luckier than most. Born into an affluent family with connections, it had been easy to make his social media account one that people would follow. He was doing stuff most people could only dream of. But Lila wasn't *most* people.

"Don't worry. Tomorrow we will go shopping and—"

"I have a meeting at ten," she reminded him.

He normally didn't get up until well after ten, but

just nodded. "Not a problem. Afterward, we will get your new wardrobe. I have some friends—other influencers—who do glam for me and I asked them to come to Royal and give you a few tips."

"Glam? Zach, I'm not glamorous, and I think everyone in town will be shocked if I start dressing like this every day."

"Why?" he asked. "You're wearing a pretty summer dress, not haute couture. Is it that you won't be comfortable?"

She tipped her head to the side. "Do we know each other well enough to have this kind of conversation?"

"We don't. But I've always found that deep subjects are better discussed with strangers."

Lila nodded and looked away again, back out at the bay. He had the feeling he'd disappointed her. *Get used to it, honey,* his subconscious jeered. He shut down that annoying inner voice. But the thought lingered. He knew that as much as he might say that he liked to keep moving, a part of him had learned early on that he wasn't good in relationships.

A part of him felt like that stemmed from his father. The old man couldn't commit, and neither could Zach. But another part knew being a bad boy just worked for his brand. Kept him on target and raking in the money.

"I only meant it's easier to unload your secrets when you have no agenda. And usually with strangers there isn't one. You don't have any expectations from me…other than helping you promote your event."

She looked back at him and her brown eyes seemed a little nervous. "I don't like being the center of attention. I'm sure that's not a shock to you. I took the job at the Royal Chamber of Commerce because I love my community. But I usually work behind the scenes."

"And you thought this would be another behind-the-scenes role?"

"Yes, and let's be honest—my role is definitely behind-the-scenes," she murmured. "It's you and your dare making me step out of the shadows. I never expected to be doing this."

"Do you want to stop? Go back to your old self?" he asked. "You haven't done anything except get tagged in a photo with me."

"I know that." She sighed. "But I have to admit I like it. Those women in the lobby asked about the event and were ready to book tickets… This is the kind of promo I was hoping to generate."

Their food arrived before she could say anything else and he noticed her phone was still blowing up with notifications and text messages. She looked at it and then smiled.

"What is it?"

"Nothing. Everyone on the committee has noticed the likes. I think I'm going to have to keep doing this. But if I do, we need to establish some ground rules," she said.

He took a bite of his sea bass, nodding at her and trying to figure out what kind of rules she was talking about. Like missionary position only? He had the feeling she'd be more adventurous in bed, but knew that wasn't what she'd meant. His mind was just going to filthy places.

"Like what?"

"You can't buy me clothes. I'm not comfortable with that. I will pay you back for this… It might be in installments, but I *have* to pay you back," she insisted.

"Fine. But the truth is, we won't be paying for many of your clothes," he said. "Usually stores and labels gift them to me as long as I tag them in the photos. And it will work the same for you."

"How does that make them money?" she asked curiously.

"Well, all of your followers are going to want to be like you," Zach explained. "So we tag the brands, the shop you purchased it in, and then we let the likes and human nature do the rest. People will start snapping up the items. You'll be gifted more stuff than you have ever imagined."

She shook her head, that high ponytail swinging with the motion, drawing his eye to the long, graceful line of her neck. "All because of a few pictures?"

"No. All because of your image and your influence. That's how you are going to wow your followers and make them want to meet you at Soiree on the Bay."

Just like she was wowing him with her honesty and charming him with her smile, he thought. Now he needed to step up his game and start wowing *her*.

Lila stopped worrying after her second glass of champagne. It was so delicious, she started to wonder why she didn't drink it more often. Zach suggested a walk along the pier at the marina after their meal and looped her arm through his as they walked. She tipped her head back and looked up at the stars in the night sky. It was so vast and clear tonight.

She watched them twinkling and then caught her breath as she saw a shooting star. She made a quick wish that this night would be as magical as she felt it was in this moment.

"What is it?" he asked.

"Shooting star. Quick…make a wish!"

He didn't look up at the sky as he stopped walking but turned and looked down into her eyes. "I wish for one kiss."

She gazed up at him. His thick eyebrows, the tanned skin and the full mouth that easily smiled. *One kiss.*

She wanted that, too, on this night. With him. It had been so long since she'd wanted a man. She had been on dates and even slept with a few guys in the last year or so. But honestly, it had been more just to get out of the house. It hadn't felt like *this*.

Her rational mind shouted it was the champagne

and the moonlight, but she didn't care. She wanted that kiss as much as he did.

She put her hand on the side of his jaw, felt the rough abrasion of his stubble, and then he turned his head and kissed the center of her palm. A shiver ran up her arm and her breasts felt fuller, her heart beat faster again and everything feminine inside her seemed to wake up and say, *Yes, girl, let's get some more of this guy.*

"There's your kiss," she said.

"Damn."

She looked up at him from under her eyelashes and shook her head. "You missed."

"I did?"

"Yes, you did," she whispered, going up on tiptoe, balancing herself with her hand on his shoulder and kissing him.

The first brush of her lips against his was everything she'd hoped it would be and more. The giddy butterflies in her stomach took flight and she brought her other hand to the back of his neck, pushing her fingers up into the thick hair at the back of his head.

His hand was on her waist, pulling her into his body, and his chest was solid against her torso. He lifted her slightly and then shifted so that his back was to the walkway, keeping them from prying eyes.

As he leaned down over her, she felt his lips part and his tongue brush over hers. She sighed. He tasted so good. Of champagne and that minty thing he'd had for dessert. His arms around her were solid and she clung to him, realizing how easy it would be to fall under his spell. She pulled back and looked up at him. Something shifted inside her and she wondered if she'd be here in his arms if she hadn't agreed to his makeover.

Ugh.

She hated that notion. Where were these thoughts coming from?

The smart part of the brain and not the hoo-hah, her subconscious reminded her.

Stop.

"What is it?"

"Would you have kissed me if I was still wearing my regular clothes?" she asked.

Oh, great, now she decided to start dropping truth bombs instead of enjoying the champagne glow of the evening.

"Yes. I wanted to kiss you in the doorway of the chamber of commerce building when you first ran into me."

Was he lying?

She realized she didn't know him well enough to be able to judge the truth from the lies. And did it matter? Deep conversations, like white-hot sex, were probably best exchanged between strangers. Or at least that was her experience. The hot flame of lust often didn't last in relationships and it had been a really long time since… Was she going to let this chance slip away?

"What are you thinking, Lila? No woman has ever looked at me the way you do," he confessed.

She put her hand on the side of his face again because she liked touching him. Liked the feel of his stubble against her palm. Liked the way he met her gaze squarely and didn't hide from her. Liked…him.

Danger, girl.

She knew it was dangerous. Didn't need her subconscious to warn her. Zach wasn't a stranger to her anymore. He was starting to become real. She already wasn't sure how she was going to work with him and still keep her head straight. Now she was kissing him in the moonlight and making wishes on stars that weren't sensible.

"Lila?"

"I was just wishing that this was real. That this night wasn't just magic and make-believe," she said softly. The words meant as a reminder to herself but ones that she was struggling to make herself heed.

He quirked a brow. "Why isn't it real?"

"Really, ZB? You know why. I'm your flavor of the moment, and don't shake your head and pretend it's anything else."

"I wasn't going to. What's wrong with that?"

"Nothing," she told him. "If I was really the girl in that selfie you snapped. But I'm still me inside."

He stepped back, nodding his head a few times and putting his hands on his hips. "You're you on the outside, too. You just haven't adjusted to the new look and the new attitude. I can wait until you do."

"What if I never do?"

"Then we will have had this one kiss in the moonlight, and I will count myself a lucky man," he said.

Her heart wanted to melt but that stubborn part of her psyche pointed out that he was good at making people believe what he said. She needed to remember that.

Five

"So how exactly are we getting home?" she asked as they walked back to the restaurant and met the Uber he'd called.

"I thought we'd take a helicopter," he said as the driver took them to the small airport and helipad where the chopper he'd rented waited.

"Really? I've never been on one. I mean, I've wanted to, but oh, my gosh. Is it scary?"

He shook his head, smiling at her. "Not scary… unless you're afraid of heights. I should have checked first. Are you?"

"No. Not at all," she said. "My parents took a helicopter tour in Hawaii for their twenty-fifth wedding anniversary. I have been wanting to try it, too."

"Then I'm glad I booked it," he told her.

Soon they were seated with their padded head-phones on and the helicopter lifted off. Lila grabbed his hand as it did so. Squeezing his fingers.

"Are you okay?" he asked.

"Yes," she replied, her voice full of excitement. "Sorry about that."

She let his hand go and then leaned toward the window to look out as the pilot took them over Trinity Bay and Mustang Point.

"It's so pretty from up here."

"It is," Zach said, but he was looking at her. He realized that he might have made a colossal mistake by waging this bet with her. He thought he was making her into a woman who could run her own brand campaign, but he knew it was more. His jaw flexed. Was he trying to make up for the sin he'd committed in Los Angeles?

A part of him wanted to play it like he was too jaded to care if he'd slept with another man's wife, but he knew he wasn't. Helping Lila wasn't going to erase that mark on his soul, but it would give him something positive to focus on. He knew he wasn't one to just use someone for his own gain…and while he liked to live life on the edge, deep down he'd always felt like he was a fairly decent person.

Lila was helping to give him a bridge back to that.

But at what cost?

"Oh, wow. I love this! The sky is even bigger up here," she said.

"It is," he agreed. She kept up a running commentary over the different sights they passed and he listened to her. He'd given her this. To him this was just a quicker way of getting from place to place. But to Lila this was an *experience*. He let that thought settle in his mind. What would she do if he took her on his private jet?

She'd probably be over the moon. But this was also a reminder of how different they were. There was an innocence to Lila that he didn't want to ruin. Yet wasn't that inevitable?

Making her over was just step one in creating a new Lila. The kind of Lila who would easily fit in and thrive in the spotlight the way he did. He wanted that for her. But he also liked it for himself, too. Helping people like Lila find their own brand and style had always appealed to him. She grabbed his leg as the lights of Royal came into view. "I can see the chamber building from here. I always knew Royal was a beautiful city, but seeing it all lit up makes it even more magical."

They landed at the helipad in the neighborhood where the house he'd rented earlier was, while she'd been getting changed. There was a golf cart waiting to take them to the house. He tipped the pilot and then led Lila to the golf cart.

"Whose house is this?"

"Mine. I rented it."

"What?" she said, her eyes widening. "I thought

you'd be heading back out of town as soon as you made a few posts about the event."

"I'm not ready to leave yet," he told her.

"Why not?"

"Well, I have to finish helping you pick out your wardrobe, and I want to meet the rest of the advisory committee," he said. "Find out a little more of your world."

She twirled a long strand of her hair around her finger as she tipped her head to the side to stare at him. "My world? It's not as exciting as anything we've done tonight. It's just sitting on the back porch listening to the fountain my dad helped me install in the backyard and reading one of my favorite books. Or going to a night class at the community center and learning how to make origami birds."

There was a note in her voice that didn't sound dismissive. Lila liked those things. She liked that quiet pace, he could tell. He wondered if, in his selfishness to make it okay for him to go after her, he'd lured her into a bargain she might regret. But would that make it his fault? As she'd said, she was a grown-ass woman.

"I'll be the judge of that," he said. "Do you need to go home now? Or do you have time for a nightcap?"

She seemed to debate her answer, sitting next to him in the golf cart in front of his house. There were two cars in the drive. His Ferrari and an Audi sedan that the driver he'd hired would use. He was a brand ambassador for Audi, so the car had been sent over from the local dealer.

"I don't think I should drink another thing tonight. Like I said, I have work in the morning and then I have the meeting with the advisory committee on Friday," she said. "I'll let them know you want to attend."

"Good. Then I will have my driver take you home."

"You have a driver?"

"Yes. I have an entire team," he answered.

She rolled her eyes at that.

"I hope you will forgive me, but I did order a few things for you to wear to the office tomorrow." He flashed a grin. "And FYI…you're all mine after your 10 a.m. meeting."

Her gaze shot to his. "I—I am?" she stammered.

"Yes, you are. I am taking you to Dallas for a shopping spree in the afternoon."

"I can't…"

"Why, do you have something scheduled?" he asked.

"No. But—"

"We made a deal. Five hundred likes in an hour and you put yourself in my hands."

"I put my *wardrobe* in your hands," she reminded him pertly.

He winked at her. He wanted all of her in his hands. "Of course. That's what I meant."

"Oh, good," she said. "Can't we go shopping here in Royal?"

"We could, but then your friends and family would be around. I thought you'd be more comfortable in Dallas."

She nibbled her lower lip, which just made him remember how soft her mouth had been under his and how much he wanted another kiss. One hadn't been enough.

Five hundred likes on one picture was what he'd used to buy that kiss, and he wondered how many likes it would take for her transformation to be complete. For her to suddenly be like him.

"Okay. Yes. We can do that. Can we take your helicopter again?"

"Yes. Meet me here after your meeting," he said.

Lila had a restless night's sleep dreaming of Zach and that hot kiss they'd shared. She'd wanted more but at the same time, this situation was reminiscent of that time she'd changed her looks for a man and been burned by him. She shook off those thoughts. Zach wasn't using her. If anything, she was using him—for work.

Stay focused, she reminded herself.

There were several packages waiting on her front porch step, all from Neiman Marcus. Her mom, who lived two streets over from Lila, had come by for coffee and to find out all about Zach. The last thing she wanted to do was have a chat about a guy she still wasn't sure about.

But as her mom helped her bring in all the boxes, she knew she was going to have to tell her something.

"I made a silly bet with him and that's what this is," she said as her mom watched her opening all the boxes.

"What kind of bet? You're normally not a gambler."

Her mother sounded concerned. Lila hoped she wasn't remembering Peter and that disastrous time she had tried to make herself into a different woman for him. The only thing that would make this embarrassing was to have to discuss that and what was happening with Zach. Or maybe it would help. Make her have to focus on how this situation was different.

For one thing, she wasn't changing anything to please him. It was for herself. Truly she liked the way that she'd felt in the new outfit Zach had selected yesterday.

So as long as it felt right, she thought her mother would be okay with this.

"I know, Mom. He said that I wouldn't need him to promote our event if I started using my social media accounts in a different way. He said he could get me over five hundred likes in an hour if I just changed my clothes and took a selfie with him."

"And he did it, didn't he?"

"Yes. But now he thinks if I just keep doing this, taking photos of myself…" She cringed. "Oh, Mom, what have I gotten myself into?"

Her mom had gotten up and was helping her open

all of the packages with an amused smile on her face. She pulled out a cute, trendy outfit and held it up. "I don't know, but I like it. This is the first time I've seen you…well, excited about a boy."

Boy.

Ha.

Zach wasn't a boy. He was a total superhot man as evidenced by the steamy dreams that he'd starred in last night. She almost blushed and turned away because she knew her mom would notice. "It's not him per se as much as it is…just the thought of doing something new."

"Good. Do you want this change?"

Her mother always had a way of asking the shrewd questions that Lila tended to avoid answering to herself.

"I think I do. I really liked the way I felt yesterday, it was fun, and when I saw myself in the mirror—it was like I was the girl I see in my head, you know what I mean?"

"I do," she said. "And there is nothing wrong with dressing up and liking what you see. You've always seemed to shy away from all of this. Just make sure you haven't made this decision for someone else."

She shook her head. "Of course not. I think this will help with my job, which you know I love. And the Soiree, which I want to be a success."

"Then great. I love it. Wish I could stay and watch you try on all these clothes, but your father booked us an earlier tee time than normal. I swear, that man is trying to make me crazy now that he's retired," her mom said with a smile as she kissed her on the top of the head and ran out the door after saying goodbye.

Lila watched the door close behind her and then looked back at all the clothes. She was still young but there was a part of her that wanted the loving partnership her parents had found. While she knew there had been a lot of ups and downs between them and she was very happy in her single life, there was something to be said for sharing a life with another person.

Of course, she probably needed to figure herself out before she tried a relationship, she thought.

Which led her right back to the fashionable new wardrobe awaiting her. Her mom had been support-ive—honestly, she and her dad always were—and Lila knew she was blessed to have that kind of fam-ily. But she'd also been right when she'd said this kind of change couldn't be for likes or for followers. It had to be for herself.

Lila sighed. She wasn't like Zach, who moved blithely through the world, changing looks and lov-ers with the seasons and trends.

No matter how exciting that helicopter ride and her mini photo shoot had been, that wasn't real. Royal was real. She pulled the bright-colored de-signer outfit that had caught her eye out of the tissue and took it with her to get ready for her day. This was the kind of thing she'd have purchased for herself if she had the money. So she felt no guilt in wearing it.

She left the house, her hair once again in a high ponytail because she hadn't had time to do anything else with it, and drove to the office.

"Morning, Lila."

She smiled at Josh Peterson, one of her coworkers at the chamber of commerce, and waved at him as she walked over to the coffee shop to grab her morning java. Several men and women all smiled and waved at her, even strangers. Hmm…perhaps there *was* something to dressing differently, she thought.

"What have you been up to lately?" one of the guys who'd gone to high school with her asked.

"I'm helping organize the Soiree on the Bay," she said. "Have you heard about it?"

"Rumblings. Isn't that something that Rusty Edmond and his family are putting together?"

"Yes. It's going to be *fabulous*! Check out our website for more details. Hope to see you there."

"You will. Hope to see you again before then," he said, winking at her as he walked away.

Had he been flirting? She wasn't sure. In high school he had pretty much only talked to her when he wanted to cheat off her in English.

Lila got her coffee order and then went to her desk, realizing that no matter what else had happened yesterday, Zach had given her a boost in confidence that she was definitely able to use in her job and in her life.

She wasn't going to tell him because his ego was big enough already, but these changes might have been long overdue.

* * *

Zach's crew all started arriving around ten, but he didn't get out of bed until noon normally. He'd always been a bit of an insomniac, so staying up all night and thinking about Lila and then her media presence had been a nice distraction.

He had to force himself to stop remembering how she'd felt in his arms, so instead he'd developed a plan and even sent several emails to his team to get them thinking. He wondered what she'd think about the clothes he'd had sent from Neiman Marcus and had half expected her to text him and tell him that she couldn't keep them, but she hadn't.

He had checked his phone a few times waiting for something from her and then realized what he was doing. *Likes* mattered, not people. But he'd thought she was different… Maybe she had been until he started making her over. Yeah, he knew that sounded cold but whenever he'd relied on a person…well, he'd been let down. He'd therefore learned to keep things bright and breezy. But some part of him was always sort of hoping for more.

"Hello, Mrs. Smith," he said, coming into the kitchen. His housekeeper always flew to wherever he was staying. She was fifty-six but looked younger and had been married to her high school sweetheart for three years before she'd been widowed. Mrs. Smith had no kids and said she'd learned that being married wasn't for her. She was motherly without smothering him and she knew how he liked his meals fixed. His housekeeper also had her own media account and a huge following, mainly folks who wanted to style their houses and food. She was a genius when it came to that.

"Morning, ZB. I staged your lunch at the table by the pool if you want to snap a pic before we talk about dinner. You mentioned a guest in your email. Fancy or simple Texas fare? I found a recipe from your great-granny Benning's notes that I could use."

"I like your thinking," he said. "Let me post my lunch and then we can discuss. Are the rest of the team here?"

"Vito and Dawn are. Shantal made a coffee run."

"We have coffee here," he reminded her.

"Oh, she knows, honey, but she wanted to check out Lila in person. Everyone is intrigued."

He just shook his head. He felt protective of Lila, he realized. "She's not a toy."

"Isn't she?" Mrs. Smith asked. "You kind of made it seem like she was something new and shiny for everyone to play with in all those emails."

"I'm helping her build her presence and you all can help with that. But that's it," he said. "Sorry if I sound cranky."

"It's all right, honey. Take your coffee and go do your thing."

He took the steaming mug with him and walked out onto the stone patio, which was covered with reclaimed railroad timber, spaced apart with some kind of purple flowering vine growing on them. Zach stopped and took a deep breath. It was fresh and not too sweet-smelling. He saw the area that Mrs. Smith had staged for him. As he walked to the table, the waterfall into the landscaped pool came on. The table was laid with his monogrammed tablecloth from a luxury British maker and the plates were from an exclusive designer.

He lifted the cloche off his lunch and had to smile. Mrs. Smith knew how to capture summer with her lobster rolls, coleslaw and peach iced tea. His tripod was set up from last night when he'd prepped for the day. Taking his camera out of the bag that had been left for him on the chair, he fiddled with the settings until he had the look he wanted. Then he took his seat, donned his sunglasses and stared off in the distance.

Normally he thought about his latest girlfriend or next big project, something to make him smile. Unbidden, an image of Lila just as he'd leaned in to kiss her the night before danced through his mind. He remembered the sound of her laughter and the way she'd smelled of lavender, the way her mouth had felt under his and her body pressed against his. He couldn't wait to see her again.

He hit the remote trigger for the shutter release on the camera, but he was distracted by her. Why hadn't she texted him this morning?

Had she regretted yesterday? Was she going to tell him to hit the road?

And why the hell did that matter? There were a

million other ladies waiting in the wings…well, not a *million*, but a few. If she wasn't interested in him, he'd find another woman and go back to Los Angeles, face the paparazzi and the moral police, and deal with his own conscience.

But he didn't want to just disappear. He wanted Lila. He wanted her to need his help. He was kind of addicted to her excitement and her smile. He wanted to see it again. Wanted to kiss her again. And so much more.…

Hell.

What was he thinking?

They could have fun. For a while. But this other stuff, this gnawing need deep inside him, needed to be quelled and quieted. He wouldn't let himself become obsessed with her.

She was his project…that was all. Not someone he was using; someone he was helping. That was it.

But was it ever enough? He'd helped other people and companies before but there was always something in it for him. And this Soiree thing she was planning, there wasn't anything in it for him. He was a bigger draw than anyone she'd mentioned to him so far. What did he need to feel compensated?

Her.

He wanted her. He intended to seduce her. But he knew that wasn't going to happen. She was way too smart to fall for him. He knew that. So could he just do this for her? He wasn't sure that he wasn't also doing this for himself. He'd said he liked her but just now it hit him that he wanted her to like *him*. The real him, not the million followers kind of like but the man he was away from social media.

Would that be enough?

He had no idea, but he also knew that unless she told him she didn't want his help anymore, he was going to be right here in her life for the foreseeable future.

Six

Arriving at Zach's rental house after lunch, Lila was determined to do this on her own terms. She'd talked to the rest of the festival advisory board and set up a meet and greet for them with Zach on Friday night at Sheen. Charlotte had promised them a quiet, private table at the back of the popular restaurant where they could talk. And being in the public would both suit Zach and generate publicity for the event.

Along with Charlotte, the advisory board consisted of Jack Bowden, whose company had done all of the construction at the festival site, and Valencia Donovan, a sort of bohemian cowgirl who was drop-dead gorgeous and ran the Donovan Horse Rescue. Brett Harston had also been on the committee but he was booted after a run-in with Rusty Edmond over the fact that he'd started dating Sarabeth, who was Rusty's ex-wife. There was never a stop to the drama that surrounded the Edmond family. Billy Holmes was sort of advising the advisory committee. He was a family friend of the Edmonds…well, sort of. Seemed he and Ross had been college roommates. Billy really was the only one who got the cantankerous Rusty Edmond under control, and had been overseeing the event.

The Soiree was in July, which meant she really needed to get some word-of-mouth promo that wasn't just everyone in Royal. And she'd do whatever it took to make that happen. Even if it entailed changing her image and hanging out with Zach. Her mom's words were a warning in the back of her mind about making sure the change was for herself, but for the first time since she'd been meeting with the rest of the advisory committee, she didn't feel like she was just there to take notes. Not that anyone had ever treated her that way, but today she'd felt more confident and had spoken up, telling everyone that she was in talks with documentary filmmaker Abby Carmichael, which was only half true.

The front door opened, and she realized she was still sitting in her car in front of his large house. The circular brick driveway led up to the imposing modern abode, which had large glass windows and beautiful stonework.

She saw Zach standing there—he had his sunglasses on and behind him were three people. They were crowded around him and leaned out as if to catch a glimpse of her. There was a tall guy with spiky brown hair with blond tips. A curvy woman with curly hair who waved at her. And finally, a woman who was taller than Zach with hair down to her butt. She crossed her arms over her waist and said something to the others.

This must be his team. His "glam team." Oh, goodness, what had she gotten herself into?

Confidence. That was what she'd gotten.

Get out of the car, Lila, she told herself.

She turned off the engine, grabbed the large cross-body bag that Zach hadn't loved and got out.

"Hi," she said as she walked up the drive. "Sorry about that. I was finishing up a call."

"Sure. This is Vito, Dawn and Shantal. They are on my team and will be helping you with a few tips. Have you had lunch?"

She nodded as she followed Zach and his team into the foyer of his house. It was large with marble floors and modern decor. She took a moment to look around and realized that he'd picked a place that would photograph well in his posts.

"Good. Then we get straight to it. Vito is one of the best hairdressers in the country."

"Excuse me? Did I hear that right? I'm the best in the *world*, honey," Vito said. "This man was a ragamuffin until I did his do. I mean shaggy might work for the just-from-bed posts but not for the red carpet."

She laughed with Vito as Zach just shrugged. "Sorry, V. You know I'm nothing without you."

Vito patted him on the shoulder. "That's okay, hon. So what do you want to do with her hair?"

"Nothing," she said.

He raised both eyebrows at her. As he came over he touched the length of her hair and then walked around behind her to look at the ends. "You have great hair. I have some ideas that will give you more of a modern look but keep most of your length. Is that what you meant?"

She glanced over at Zach and found him watching her. He had that same look on his face as he had last night when he'd kissed her. She couldn't help remembering how his mouth felt on hers. Was he going to kiss her again? Or had he regretted it?

"Lila?" Vito asked.

"I am really not much on fixing my hair. It takes forever to blow-dry and curling it has always…well, not worked out. I'm okay to cut some of the length. Really when I said nothing, I meant I don't want to spend an hour getting ready in the morning."

"Got it. Let me pull some photos together while you and ZB are in Dallas shopping. Highlights?"

She scrunched her nose. Her hair was dark brown with natural highlights in it. And despite the fact that this was Texas and every time she went to the salon, they suggested lightening it, she'd resisted. "I don't think so."

"Got it. Want to keep your look more you," Vito said. "This is going to be fun."

Vito dashed off up the stairs and then Shantal and Dawn both stared at her. "Dawn will help you with writing your posts and using the right hashtags. Shantal is going to do your makeup."

"I'm guessing the easier the better?" Shantal asked. She was tall with hair all the way down to her butt and had a deep timbre to her voice. Her eyes were bright green. She wore minimal makeup, but she had such lovely bone structure that honestly, she didn't need it. Her skin was a deep olive complexion and her high cheekbones and full mouth made her stunning.

"Yes, for every day. But could you also show me how to do something for going out? Right now, I just swap my lip balm for red lipstick and some mascara."

"Girl, don't worry. I'll give you a couple of different looks."

"I'll start working on some posts for you," Dawn said. "Have you taken any photos today?"

"No. Should I?"

"Yes. I know you are promoting the event, but we also want everyone to see how fun and one-of-a-kind you and Royal are. While you and ZB are shopping I'll go scout some locations and have some ideas when you come back."

Dawn and Shantal left after that.

"How are you doing? Was that too much?" he asked.

She smiled over at him. It was as if he was see-

ing the real her, the one behind all of these new fa-
cades. She wanted to just be honest with him. But
at the same time, she felt exposed now. She didn't
have her normal clothing to hide behind. If she let
him all the way in, would she regret it?

"It was a little overwhelming. Are you sure we
need all this?" she asked, though the idea of a makeover was exciting. She'd always wanted to wear more
makeup but had never been sure how to go about it.

"It is. But it will be fun. Ready to head to Dallas
with me?" he asked.

More ready than he was aware. After dreaming of
him all night, then waking up to the new clothes he'd
sent, it had been hard not to text him before coming
over today. A part of her wanted to know if he'd been
thinking about her as much as she'd been thinking
about him. Not as his pet project but as a woman.

She wrapped her arms around her waist. This was
it—she was going to have to face that fear deep inside her that she wasn't woman enough for him. No
matter how confident she was at her job, or in planning the Soiree, one-on-one with Zach, she stumbled.

"Yes," she said. She'd been looking forward to
seeing him again all day. Now that they were alone
she was both excited and a little bit scared.

"I can't believe they just gave us all of this stuff!"
Lila exclaimed as they got back on his private plane
at the small airport near Love Field.

It had taken all of his willpower to keep his hands

to himself while they'd shopped today. She'd tried on outfit after outfit and modeled them for him, her grin growing bigger each time.

She had been reluctant to hand over any of the bags of stuff that had been gifted to her. She sat on the large leather couch in the main part of the plane as the pilot and attendant got it ready for them to fly back to Royal.

They'd had dinner at a revolving restaurant that had afforded them a view of Dallas at night. Lila had gotten a like from one of the *Rich Wives* that she followed and spontaneously hugged him. He'd hugged her back, gotten a boner and realized he needed some space. So he'd stepped away from her and turned the conversation to being a brand ambassador. As if talking was going to turn him off. It hadn't worked, but she hadn't seemed to notice. Lila hadn't stopped talking since they'd gotten back on the plane.

They'd taken care of her glasses first and she now wore a pair of chic-looking frames that no longer dwarfed her face. She kept her hair in the ponytail, but some strands had slipped and now curled around her face. Her cheeks were flushed, and she kept looking at all the bags that were piled on the other couch.

"I told you. In exchange for a mention in a post and tagging them each time you wear an outfit, they don't mind writing off the price of the clothes and accessories. It's way cheaper for them to do this than to shoot a commercial or pay for print advertising."

"I know but *still*. I'm going to send thank-you notes to all of them," she said.

He almost laughed but knew she might take that the wrong way. So instead he only smiled. There was something so refreshingly innocent about her. That was what had drawn him to her in the first place. She was making him feel good just by being with her. "I'm sure they will appreciate that."

"Manners are never wasted."

"I agree," he murmured. "Also, I have a present for you. This wasn't gifted to me. I purchased it for you."

"What is it?" she asked.

He reached behind the leather armchair he was seated in and pulled the orange Hermès box out, handing it to her. She took it and put it on her lap, slowly opened the box and then pulled out the Birkin bag that he'd had monogrammed with her initials. It had an adjustable strap so she could wear it across her body as she did that hideous thing she'd been carrying all day.

She caught her breath as she stared at the high-end bag. She'd never received anything like this before. She was almost afraid to touch it.

"Zach…are you sure you want to give this to me?"

"Yes. I am positive," he told her. "I want you to transfer all of your stuff into it right now and then we can burn that other one."

"I am *not* burning my favorite bag. But thank you for this. I will start using it."

"Good," he said.

She set the box aside after they were in the air for the thirty-minute plane ride. He'd told Jennifer, the flight attendant, that she wouldn't be needed so she was sitting in the cockpit with the pilot.

"Thank you for all of this. I always thought that fashion wasn't anything but a waste of time but earlier today in a meeting…I felt more confident than I normally did. Started speaking up more. That's not what I expected."

He got up and went to sit next to her on the couch, stretching his arm along the back of it and toying with the hair in her ponytail. "I'm glad. I think we are changing the outside Lila to match the inside one."

She turned to face him, putting her hand on his thigh. "I agree. But I'm still wondering what's in this for you."

A shiver of awareness went through him. His skin felt too tight and it took all of his control to just keep from reaching over and pulling her into his arms.

"Can't I just be a good guy who is doing this because I'm nice?" he asked. But no one thought of him that way. Not even himself. He was the bad boy who kept the gossip sites and paparazzi busy following his latest scandal.

"Yes, of course. It's just that many people do that these days. I mean even the Soiree on the Bay isn't just for charity. There is a lot of money to be made by the vendors who are participating."

"I get it. But this…this is for you, Lila."

She furrowed her brow. "But you don't know me."

"What do you want me to say? That I'm using you?" he asked. Had she somehow gleaned that he wanted her to fit into his world? Honestly, he was not sure what he wanted from her. He knew he wanted her naked, writhing under him, but there was an emotional component to this he wasn't used to dealing with. Wasn't sure he *wanted* to deal with.

"I want the truth," she said, her words direct, just like she'd been from the beginning.

He stopped. This. This fire and passion. These were the things he'd sensed in her from the beginning and this was what he wanted from her. But how to show her without revealing his hand? Without allowing himself to seem too…needy?

"It was a bet. Remember? And I won. I'm not someone who reneges on a bet. That's not my style," he said. The truth was it was so much more than that. Plus it was fun watching her excitement at the new stuff and designing her new look. But just being around her aroused him. It wasn't like he needed to see her naked to get turned on.

Hell, he'd gotten a hard-on from a hug.

A *hug.*

He normally had more control and more finesse, but this was Lila and nothing was what he expected.

"You're right. But why are you sticking around?"

"I like you," he admitted gruffly. "One kiss wasn't enough for me."

"What if it was for me?" she asked.

Damn him.

Honesty, straight from those guileless big brown eyes, and he wanted to say the hell with it and grab her and pull her into his arms. But he couldn't. Because he was starting to feel things and that wasn't him. He got a rush from driving fast—acceptable feelings. He got turned on by women—especially Lila—again acceptable. He felt all gooey inside when she told him she was sending thank-you notes to the stores that they'd been gifted things from—not acceptable.

Not *him*.

Ruefully, he nodded at her. "Then I'm out of luck."

She took his hand in hers, threading their fingers together. "I like you, too, Zach, and that kiss was amazing. But I'm not sure about this kind of lifestyle. The novelty of it is fun for right now, but I think this would wear on me after a while."

And that was probably that. His lifestyle wasn't for everyone and he knew what she was saying in that super polite way of hers. It was nice while he was here in Royal, but she must have sensed what he hadn't said. That he was hiding from the world, giving the scandal time to die down. So this wasn't real. No matter how he tried to make it so in his mind.

Lila wasn't sure what she had wanted Zach to say. Something like it had started out as a bet but was much stronger now? She knew that she was wildly infatuated with him. How could she *not* be? He was funny, generous…and hot. He made her feel like she could be herself and achieve things that honestly she'd never expected.

It was so much more than the fact that he'd given her the keys to a luxurious lifestyle that she'd never thought in a million years she could be a part of. But Zach was slowly taking away the mystery of jet airline travel and high-end shopping.

She felt like Cinderella with her own ZB fairy godfather. And that was fantasy; there weren't fairy godparents in the real world. So she'd had to bring it back to reality. No matter how attracted he might be to her in the moment, that was all this could be. A *moment*.

She'd always prided herself as being someone who was grounded in reality, but she was forced to admit that she was being swayed by him. When he touched her, even accidentally, she felt a rush go through her entire body. She wanted more, wanted to fall into his arms and his life, but she had to remember that they came from two completely different places. She lived in Royal. He lived online and in LA. He'd pulled her into a world where she wasn't sure how she'd survive yet at the same time she wanted to try. He'd said he liked kissing her, but he was a playboy who changed women as often as he posted on social media, so she wasn't building a future for the two of them. But she was building a relationship in her head.

However, she couldn't help but wonder how much

of it was because of what he could do for the Soiree.
She wanted to prove herself to the Texas Cattleman's
Club members as well as to the Edmond family. Now
that she'd had a taste of how people treated her with
her new look, she knew she didn't want to be that
little unremarkable Lila from the chamber of commerce. She wanted to be noticed and taken seriously.
She'd always been smart but she'd also always been
quiet. Now she needed to *shine*.

She wanted to change more than her clothes.

She shifted on the couch and leaned over to kiss
Zach. Just to see what he'd do. She knew that it was
forward and polite ladies didn't do this. But she was
on a private plane that had a freaking bedroom in it
with a roguishly sexy bad boy. And she'd been sitting next to him like his chaste *sister*. She wanted
for once in her life to have a story that was exciting. She wanted an experience that she knew she'd
never have a chance at again when Zach walked out
of her life. And he was going to walk out of her life.

She knew that.

So she was going into this with her eyes open and
taking this for herself. For the man who'd shown her
how to be Lila 2.0.

"Lila…" He said her name slowly in that husky
tone he'd used just last night when he'd kissed her by
the bay, and she looked up into those gorgeous blue
eyes of his, waiting and wanting so much from him.
And so much for herself. She'd always told herself she

was happy and that she had the life she wanted, but she also knew that she'd been afraid to take any risks.

This was the riskiest thing she'd *ever* done. Kissing a famous bad boy on his private plane…this wasn't the Lila Jones she'd always been.

And that brush of his lips against hers was sending chills through her. The good kind that made her pulse race and her breasts feel full. Lila put her hand on his shoulder and he wrapped his hands around her waist and lifted her, pulling her onto his lap. She wound her arms around his shoulders as he deepened the kiss, his breath mingling with hers. She sucked his tongue into her mouth.

Wanting and needing more from him. This was changing from doing something risky to doing something that she'd always wanted but never been able to find for herself. She hadn't ever been this bold, she thought. Then, shifting on his lap to straddle him, she felt his erection between her legs and pushed herself against him.

Lila cradled his head in her hands and deepened the kiss even more as he cupped her butt and urged her to rock more solidly against his hard-on. She did. Waves of pleasure rippled through her as she felt one of his palms on her back, moving up and down, then he grabbed her ponytail with one hand as he pulled his mouth from hers.

She closed her eyes and realized how close she was to coming. Just from this. But she couldn't. That would be too much for this jaded, sophisticated man.

But then he kissed her neck, nibbled at her sensitive flesh. His hand was under her shirt and he whispered in her ear, his breath hot and his words turning her on with each one. She rocked harder against him, felt his solid shaft between her legs, catching her right where it felt so good.

She did it again and then he whispered into her ear. "Come for me."

And she did. She bit back a guttural sound and continued riding him until she collapsed in his arms. He held her as she rested her head on his shoulder, his hands moving languidly up and down her back.

"I want you. But not now. We will be landing soon. The team is at my place…can we go to yours?"

He was thinking through the variables and she knew he needed to figure this out for himself. As much as she might have felt like they were together in this, he wasn't. Not really. She was a temporary diversion for him. "I'd like that. I don't have protection."

"I'll take care of it."

"Don't tell me you have a sponsor for those," she said, feeling vulnerable to him at this moment. Even though she'd been the aggressor, now she was having thoughts…all kinds. Like wanting more of him and also afraid that if she had more of Zach she might not want to let him go.

"No. Definitely not. Some things are just for me and not for my public persona," he said.

Me? She didn't ask but she wanted to know. She

had the feeling that it was better not to know and instead maneuvered back into her seat as they landed in Royal.

Zach looked at her as if nothing had changed while inside she'd felt a huge shift, and maybe that was because this was his life. Things like women throwing themselves at him happened every day.

God.

What had she gotten herself into?

Seven

Lila's house was tucked into a cute neighborhood of older homes. She gave him directions in that quiet, direct voice of hers, which let him know she hadn't changed her mind. This woman was an enigma and it had been a long time since he'd allowed himself to be drawn into something like this. He stopped at a convenience store and ran in for protection along the way. Then a short time later found himself pulling into the alleyway that led to the garage at the back of her house.

"The garage door opener is in my car. Let me go inside and I'll open it for you, so you won't have to park in the driveway."

"Trying to keep me a secret?" he asked. A little

bit because he wasn't sure if she was embarrassed to sleep with him and a little bit because it sort of seemed like something she'd do. Lila was a private person by nature. He suspected she wouldn't want her neighbors to know about them.

"Yes. My mom is good friends with Mrs. Anderson, who lives one street over, and if she spots a car in my drive in the morning my mom will hightail it over here."

He wouldn't mind meeting Lila's mother but he wasn't sure the morning after was going to be the best time for that introduction. "Go on and open the door."

She hopped out of the Ferrari and opened the wooden gate on her fence. A few moments passed before he heard the garage door open, and then he pulled in and parked before getting out of the car. Her garage was super neat with metal shelving on one wall and well-labeled tubs on each shelf. She opened the door to the house and stood there watching him as she closed the garage door.

He swung his keys around on his finger and realized he was nervous about the emotions she stirred in him. Not about the sex. Sex he could handle. But nervous that the real Lila hadn't really changed enough yet. That if he slept with this woman she was going to change *him*.

"This is very organized."

"I'm sure your garage is, as well."

"Actually, it is. I have several cars that I keep in

it so it's large. I also have a driver and a mechanic back in LA who maintain everything so it's neat, but I'm not responsible."

"Fair enough," she said. "Want to come in or are you going to keep admiring my garage?"

"I want to come in…if you still want me to."

"I haven't changed my mind. Have you?" she asked. "I know I'm not your usual glam girl."

"No, you aren't." Zach was beginning to see the chink in his plan. He had been trying to change her, make her into someone who looked like the women he normally associated with, never noticing that he wasn't changing the woman inside. She was so much more than those self-absorbed women who were sort of mirror images of him. Wanting to be famous, craving some kind of influence over the world around them and seeking just the pleasure of the moment.

Lila had substance.

He had to remind himself that she was different. Because he didn't want to be the same with her as he'd been with everyone else. But could he change?

Did he really *want* to?

Or was this feeling just something new that once he'd experienced it would fade?

"So…"

"I haven't changed my mind," he reassured her.

"Then come on in, ZB," she said, stepping back and holding open the door.

ZB.

Zach walked in and put his keys on the round wood-and-tile table in the breakfast nook. A lot of lovers had called him that before, but he didn't want her to. Hell. This right here was what he'd been hoping to avoid. Maybe once they had sex he'd regain his perspective.

"Don't call me ZB. Unless... Are you hoping to have sex with ZB?" he asked.

She shook her head, her long ponytail bouncing. "No. But I'm nervous. You've had a revolving door on your bedroom forever—not judging you, but I've only had sex three times. And let's just say it was sort of beige."

"I can promise tonight won't be beige."

"Good. I'm glad to hear it. Zach, are you sure about this?"

"This? Sex or something more?" he asked.

"Sex. This can't be something more. You are not staying in Royal and I am. I want... This is fun, and you turn me on. I like who I am with you."

"Good," he said. "I like who you are with me, too."

He took off his suit jacket and hung it over the back of the chair and then toed off his shoes. Leaving them next to the same chair he'd hung his jacket on. "Give me the tour?"

"The tour? Sure. It's not fancy like your place."

"You're not me, so I wouldn't expect it to be," he said, putting his hand on the small of her back as she turned. She'd said she was nervous and that bothered him. Sex should be fun, hot, exciting…no place for nerves. He knew he was going to have to put her at ease and luckily, he was good at that.

She sort of half turned so that her shoulder brushed against his chest and then she put her soft, delicate hand on him. "This is the kitchen… I was really excited about the double ovens when I saw this place and pretty much that's why I bought it."

"Double ovens?"

She sighed. "I like to bake. This way I can do bread in one oven and cookies or cakes in the other."

He leaned down closer to her as she tipped her head back and their eyes met. She was shy about her life around him, and he knew that was his fault. He'd pointed out how her social media stream made her seem, well, boring. But he knew she was anything but.

He rubbed his thumb over her cheek and knew he had to keep his guard up with her. She was already making him think and feel things that were unexpected. He wondered if he would need reminding that this was just sex.

Because when she talked about baking and he looked at her sweet, cozy house, he realized that she'd stirred some long-forgotten dream in the back of his mind. So much of Lila was tied to Royal and when she talked about the town, she made him see it through her eyes. A dream that was foreign and not his reality. But when he was holding this beautiful woman in his arms, he craved it.

* * *

Lila's nerves dissipated as soon as Zach touched her. She'd never been wishy-washy about what she wanted. And she definitely wanted Zach. The more time she spent with him the more dimensions she was coming to realize he had. He was so much more than the bad boy with the millions of followers on social media. He was complex and caring. Charming and sexy. And way more real than she'd have expected.

There was something so solid about him, and while showing him her kitchen wasn't exactly what she'd had in mind when she'd invited him back to her place, it was giving her the time she needed to shake off the lingering anxiety that had been plaguing her since she'd realized that her neighbors might see his car.

Not that she cared what anyone else thought.

But so much of her time with Zach had been played out in the spotlight that she wanted this night just for the two of them.

He leaned in and she could smell the mint on his breath that she'd seen him pop in his mouth when they'd gotten off the plane. He had the softest lips but his mouth was firm. Out of all the men she'd kissed he was the best. And there was something about how his mouth moved over hers that made her stop thinking and just want to let herself go.

He kissed her slowly, as if there were no time and nothing existed outside of her and him and this moment. And for the first time in her life, she shut off the running list inside her mind. Instead, she put her hand on the side of his neck, her fingers brushing the thick hair at the back of his head.

She didn't have to hurry through this in case he came to too quickly or changed his mind. Zach wasn't going anywhere tonight. Tonight he was hers and she wanted to use every moment of that time. Experience everything he had to give her.

He put his arm around her waist and pulled her more fully into his body. Lila felt his strength as his biceps flexed and he turned until he was leaning against the island in the middle of her kitchen. She was sort of reclining on him, her arms around his neck, her breasts pillowed on his chest and her hips resting against him.

She felt his erection against the bottom of her stomach and she remembered that shirtless picture of him that she'd seen when scrolling through his social media feed. He was totally ripped…swole in the best way possible. And she wanted to see him naked in her kitchen.

She stepped back and he raised both eyebrows at her.

"Would you mind taking off your shirt? I want to see if you look as good in real life as you do in your photos."

He threw his head back and laughed as his hands went to the buttons of his shirt. "I look better."

She bet he did. There was no shame in Zach and he undid the buttons of his shirt with a casual elegance that turned her on as she watched those long fingers moving down the front of his body. He let the sides hang open, giving her a tantalizing glimpse of his rock-hard abs and muscled pectorals as he undid the cuffs. And then he shrugged out of his shirt and once again walked over to one of the kitchen chairs and draped it carefully over the back.

He turned to face her. Putting one hand on his hip as he stood there. Flexed and waiting. "What do you think?"

"Me-ow!" she said. "You *are* better in person."

"Yeah, because you can touch me."

"I can," she murmured, walking over to him. His expensive cologne was subtle and delicious, she thought, breathing in the scent. She reached out to touch him, drawing her finger over the pads of muscles on his chest. His flat, brown nipples hardened as she drew her finger over his skin. He had a light dusting of hair on his chest and she brushed her fingers over it, following the path over his abs and to his belt buckle.

She noticed the bulge against the front of his pants and reached down to stroke him through the fabric. He reached for the button at the back of the halter top she wore and she felt him undo it before he drew the hem of the blouse up and over her head. Then he folded it in half and set it on the table next to them.

He touched her then. Using his forefinger, drawing it down over her collarbone, following the lacy fabric of her bra as he skimmed his touch over the globes of her breasts and then lower over her stomach to her belly button, where she had a piercing. He fondled the diamond stud she had there.

"This is surprising."

"I guess there is a lot about me you don't know," she said. But she was the first to admit that she wasn't at her wittiest right now. Her heart was beating faster and faster with anticipation and really all she wanted to do was get naked and feel him moving inside her.

"Babe, you're not telling me the news. I think I could spend a month of nights with you and still not have you figured out."

Ditto. But this wasn't about figuring each other out. This was about being young and living in the moment instead of always trying to be the smart, sensible woman.

She took his hand in hers. "Want to see the master bedroom?"

"Yes," he said, following her as she led him through the formal living room to her bedroom.

Lila's bedroom was large and decorated in the same cozy style as the rest of her house. She had a queen-size sleigh bed with a summer-patterned quilt on it. Next to the bed was a table with an antique lamp and over the headboard was a photograph of Texas bluebonnets in a field. She had hit the overhead light when they came into the room and the ceiling fan turned on with it. She had a hope chest at the end of her bed.

The room smelled of gardenias. She toed off her shoes and then reached for the side zipper of her pants and let them slide down her thighs. He stopped looking around her room, fixated by her long legs, her curvy hips and the tiny bikini underwear that matched the icy green bra she still wore. She had a nipped-in waist and a small pouch of a stomach, but she was fit and she was clearly comfortable with her body.

He took the box of condoms he'd picked up and tossed them on the bed behind her while he removed his socks and then undid his belt and looked around for someplace to put his clothes. Opting to just drop them on the floor, he flung them down, then stalked toward Lila, taking her in his arms. He skimmed his hands down her back and felt the goose bumps on her skin as he caressed her.

Her fingers were chilly against his chest as she ran them down his stomach and he felt her fingers at the button of his pants. She undid it and then the zipper followed a moment later and they fell down his legs. He didn't wear underwear, which he could tell surprised her as she gasped when she touched his naked erection.

She tipped her head back and he took her mouth again as she wrapped her hand around his shaft, stroking him. He undid the clasp of her bra and then tugged the garment from her body before pulling her back into his arms. He felt her hard nipples against his chest and she shifted her torso, wriggling against him. He reached down, pushing his hands inside the back of her bikini panties to cup her naked butt, lifting her off her feet and rubbing his hard-on against her.

Then he turned, walking backward until he felt the edge of her mattress against the back of his thighs, and sat down on the bed. She stood there in front of him, lips swollen from his kisses, her chest rising and falling with each breath she took. Then she pushed her underwear down her thighs and stepped out of them as he reached for the box of condoms and put one on.

She licked her lips as she watched him and he groaned, feeling himself harden even more. He reached for her hip, pulled her toward him. "Straddle me."

She did. He groaned as he felt her warm, hot center rubbing over his abdomen and then over his shaft. He held her butt in his hands and pulled her toward him as he shifted his hips until he was poised at the entrance of her body. She put her hands on his shoulders and their eyes met and something electric passed between them. That he hadn't been expecting, but she smiled at him as she straddled him, slowly lowering herself until he was deep inside her. He pulled her head to his and thrust his tongue deep in her mouth as she started moving up and down.

He let her set the pace for as long as he could

but soon her thrusts weren't enough and he needed more. Needed to be deeper inside her. He shifted back on the bed.

"Wrap your legs around me," he commanded.

She did and he lay back and then rolled over so she was under him. Lila raised both eyebrows at him and he could tell she was going to say something, but he couldn't talk. Not now. Now he needed to have every part of her. He took her mouth with his. Then he cupped her breasts, flicking his thumb over her nipple as he drove himself deeper and deeper into her.

She clung to him, her nails digging into his back as she arched under him. And he kept thrusting, propelling them both higher and higher until she tore her mouth from his and screamed his name as her body started to tighten around his. He pounded into her harder and deeper until his orgasm washed over him and he collapsed against her. Careful to brace himself on his arms so he didn't crush her.

She wrapped her arms and legs around him and held him to her until their hearts stopped racing. Then he rolled to his side and pulled her close. Cradling her against him, he stroked her back. And as she ran her finger in a random pattern over his body, and he found himself listening to the sound of her breathing, a feeling of peace washed over him.

She didn't say anything, which was telling, he thought. She always had something to say and he wondered if it was a good or a bad thing. But he was afraid to find out.

He who had never let anything scare him was afraid of what he'd see when he looked in Lila's eyes. When had she wielded this power over him? He hadn't remembered giving it to her.

He was fixing her. She was his project.

She propped her chin on her fist and looked up into his eyes, and he realized that no matter what he'd been telling himself, tonight had been about more than sex. And he had no idea what to do about that.

Eight

Lila woke up alone in her bed the next morning. She knew she shouldn't be surprised and told herself that she was cool with it. But she knew she wasn't. She had a text from Zach on her phone telling her he looked forward to seeing her later that morning when she met with the glam squad.

She read the message several times, looking for some nuance that she might be missing, but the truth was she was a little pissed that he'd left and simply texted her. Why didn't he stay?

Oh, hell. How was she going to get to work? She'd left her car at Zach's place. This was…a mess. She had a feeling she was going to have to call her parents and ask them to give her a ride.

No.

That wasn't happening. She wasn't going to call them.

Coffee first, then she'd figure this out.

When she got to the kitchen there was a pastry box on the counter next to a ZB coffee mug and a handwritten note.

> *You were sleeping so solidly I didn't want to wake you, but I figured you needed your car— it's in your garage. Also you probably didn't want the neighbors to see me leaving. Wish I could be here with you to share these croissants.*
> *ZB*

Well…okay. So maybe he wasn't a total douche-bag. Lila opened the box and saw there were two freshly made croissants. She put the pod in to make her coffee and went to check for her car, which was in her spot. Her keys were on the breakfast table, so she knew he'd taken them to bring it back.

That was a lot of work for early in the morning. It was a nice gesture and she tried not to read too much into it but he'd totally changed her Friday from manic and crazy to a good one. She ate the buttery croissant, which was delicious with her coffee, and then got ready for the day.

She was smiling as she left her house and realized that Zach was responsible for today's good mood. It wasn't just the fact that she was wearing the new clothes that he'd helped her pick out the day before and…damn. Was she supposed to take a photo of the breakfast? Or the outfit? She was going to need some advice. She phoned her office and told them she'd be out until lunchtime at a meeting and drove to Zach's place.

The guard at the gated community had to check before he let her in but then he cleared her and she drove to the house. She realized that maybe she should have called first but honestly, she knew she needed to start putting all of Zach's efforts to good use. And she also needed a checklist. Some sort of routine so she did all the things she was supposed to.

She rang the doorbell and an older lady she hadn't met the day before answered the door.

"Hello, you must be Lila. I'm Mrs. Smith, Zach's housekeeper. I wasn't sure when to expect you," she said.

"I hope I'm not too early. But I ate those delicious croissants and then worried that maybe I was supposed to photograph them…"

Mrs. Smith started laughing. "Welcome to my world. Glad you liked the pastries. I miss Paris. Normally we go there in the spring. So I made the dough yesterday and whipped up a batch this morning."

"You *made* them? Wow, can you show me how? Is it hard? My mom would literally die if I made homemade croissants," Lila said.

"I can. But not today. I think you are scheduled for hair and makeup and—"

"Everything, Mrs. S," Zach said, coming down the stairs. She couldn't help but remember how it had felt to be in his arms last night. This morning, he looked perfectly put together in his designer suit, body-fitting shirt and no tie. He smiled when he saw her, but she noticed that he hesitated when he reached the bottom of the steps.

She smiled back. She wondered if he felt as unsure of how they moved forward as she did. But then reminded herself this was Zach Benning…ZB…the bad boy who always knew what he was doing. Even when he was doing her? She didn't want to cheapen herself or what they'd shared, but was it just fun or did he have some other motivation?

Ugh.

Why was she having all these doubts this morning?

"Good morning, Lila," he said, kissing her on the cheek and whispering in her ear, "You look gorgeous."

"Morning, Zach," she murmured back, looking into his eyes and realizing that she felt way too vulnerable. Even in these new clothes.

"Come on. Vito wants to show you some hairstyles and then get to work. I'm afraid Shantal is like me and doesn't usually stir before noon, so she'll be down later."

Mrs. Smith disappeared, Lila assumed to the kitchen to make more fabulous food, and she followed Zach down the hall to a side room where Vito and Dawn were drinking coffee and chatting. They both looked up when she walked in and she wondered if they knew that Zach had spent the night at her place.

Someone would have had to drive back over with her car… She took a deep breath. She had to be like Zach. Like these new clothes projected. A woman who didn't worry about who knew what and just lived her life.

Yeah, she'd do that.

"So glad you are here," Vito said. "I have a couple of options for you. Ready to get started?"

"As I'll ever be," she answered, removing her bag from her shoulder. Zach took the Birkin he'd given her and winked at her as he put it on the settee.

"Love this bag."

"Thanks. It's a bit showy but so is the man who gave it to me."

He threw back his head and laughed and for the first time that morning, Lila felt like she was where she needed to be. She was herself again.

"Let's do this."

Zach sat on the settee with Dawn discussing upcoming ad campaigns that he'd agreed to do, sipping a mimosa and trying to ignore Lila and Vito. He hadn't slept a wink last night but that was his normal so no biggie, right? Except as he'd held her he'd felt a new kind of longing awaken in him. Which was definitely not his normal, so it had weirded him out.

So there he was with too much time on his hands and too many thoughts in his mind. He'd gotten out of her bed and her house and driven around Royal, which wasn't that busy at three in the morning.

Nothing was clearer as he'd driven so he'd taken care of getting her car back to her place and dropping off breakfast. Still, all of that busy work hadn't changed the fact that he still couldn't get Lila off his mind. And that was disturbing because usually he was thinking about himself.

He made no bones about being a truly self-absorbed man. It was one of his key strengths and had brought him his entire career. So he wasn't going to be apologetic about it. Everyone around him knew he was always thinking about himself. Except this morning he kept getting distracted by *her*.

"I went ahead and created some branding for Lila's page and took a stab at updating the Soiree graphics as well," Dawn said. "They used a pretty decent font on the webpage, so I just tweaked the kerning to make the letters look the same but unique. I think it should work. I'll use it for your account when you post about the event."

"Great," he replied, taking another sip of the mimosa and admitting to himself that he wished it were later in the day so he could have a real drink. That might clear Lila from his head and allow him to get back to worrying about himself for a change.

"ZB? You okay?" Dawn asked.

He turned to face her. "What? Of course I am. When have you ever known me not to be?"

"Um…well, you know that Candi's husband is tweeting about you…"

"I blocked him," Zach said. He wasn't going to have a flame war on social media about an extra-marital affair. "He sounds like a lunatic."

"Agreed. Want me to try to…" She trailed off.

"Exactly. What can you do? I already told him when he punched me outside the club, I didn't know she was married. There's nothing else to do. Let's ignore it. If he tweets about me again, I'll just say talk to your wife."

"ZB…"

"Yes?"

"Nothing. If you want me to help out let me know."

Dawn wouldn't post a cutting message like that and he didn't want her involved in something this seedy. What was wrong with him lately? First, he slept with Candi and got punched by her husband. Then Lila. Maybe that was why he was obsessed with her. She wasn't Candi; she was different.

But so far making her over hadn't stopped him from falling for her, and sex had just made him more aware of her.

"I need to make a call," he said, getting up and leaving Dawn and Vito with Lila.

He walked down the hall to the office area in the house, where he'd asked for his favorite desk and chairs to be flown in and set up. Mrs. Smith had taken care of arranging everything yesterday and the room was almost a mirror of his office in Malibu. But there was no sea view and he knew he was in Texas.

What had Grandfather seen in this place? He wondered if he got in touch with his roots...then what? He'd suddenly be a better person?

Because he knew deep down that was what was bothering him about Lila. There was no way he could be good enough for her. And he was changing her to make her more like him. Was that a conscionable thing to do? And did it really matter to him if it was? He had always taken what he wanted. Why was Lila different?

Did he want to know? Fuck. No. He didn't want to know unless somehow it helped him get back to himself.

He picked up the phone and let everyone know he'd be back in Los Angeles in one week's time. Enough of Royal. He should be done making Lila over by then and once he was back in his world— throwing parties and attending media events—he'd be back to himself.

It was just *this* place that had him all out of sorts.

"Zach?"

He glanced up and caught his breath. Lila stood in the doorway. Vito had taken a few inches off the length and it now curled around her shoulders. The hairdresser had also gotten rid of the heavy fall of bangs on her forehead and swept them aside. She didn't have any makeup on but she looked beautiful.

He stood up and walked around his desk, drawn to her as he'd been drawn to nothing else in this life. He stopped as that thought entered his head and straightened his suit jacket and started to assess her. The outfit she wore today was Dolce & Gabbana; her hair was perfect. But it was the woman he saw in her eyes that really got to him like a gut punch.

"Vito did a great job. I like it. Once Shantal shows you some makeup tips, you'll be Insta-ready."

She furrowed her brow as she stared at him. "I like it, too. It's pretty easy to do. What do you think? Is it more me?"

It *was* more her. But the Lila Jones he was turning her into made him suddenly unsure whether he should have started doing this in the first place. He felt like all the worst epithets that had ever been hurled at him.

But he ignored that.

Enough with this bleeding-heart nonsense.

"It is more you. Dawn has been working on some posts for you, and a font. Go and check in with her. I'll be back in a few minutes," he said. "I have some work to finish."

Lila caught a glimpse of herself in the ornate mirror in the hallway as she left Zach's office. She stopped and stared at herself. Wow. She looked so different. It was hard to believe that just taking a few inches off the length of her hair had made it feel so much lighter, allowing it to curl naturally around her shoulders in soft waves. Vito had added some product and shown her how to do it but he assured her it shouldn't take her too much time or effort.

This woman…she was someone that Lila had always wanted to see looking back at herself, and yet at the same time, someone different. Not better, just more comfortable about showing the world who she was. Before she'd had confidence, but now she was *owning* her space and not fading into the background. On the contrary, she was finally enabling everyone to take notice of her. But the one person she truly wanted to see her had done the complete opposite. She thought about how Zach had dismissed her from his office. He was already doing her so many favors that she hated to quibble, but yeah, it had stung.

She went back and rapped on the open door frame before walking back in. He was staring intently at his laptop but looked up as she entered the room. She cleared her throat.

"I wanted to make sure you remembered we are meeting the advisory committee tonight at Sheen," she said. "I know you don't want to miss that."

"I don't. I'll pick you up. Wear that vintage Chanel dress we got yesterday."

"I was thinking of wearing the Balenciaga pants with the halter top," she told him. "I like the silhouette it creates."

He smiled at her. "I like it, too. But the dress will show off your legs and make everyone in the restaurant take notice. It's up to you, of course."

Of course.

"Thanks for letting me know I can choose my own clothes," she said sardonically. It hadn't escaped her that Zach was different today. She was trying not to let her own doubts cloud her judgment, but a part of her wondered if he was losing interest now that they'd had sex.

"Every choice is yours," he replied. "I am just here to help you navigate and build your social presence."

She stepped into the room and closed the door behind her. "What's up with you, Zach? Last night you were different. More open. Today it's like you see yourself as the mastermind directing all my moves."

He stood up and walked around the desk. Leaning back on it, bracing one arm on the surface, caused his suit jacket to fall open and revealed the powerfully muscled chest under the dress shirt. Her mouth went dry. Immediately she remembered him naked and what it had been like to kiss him. Caress him. Make hot, passionate love to him…

"I don't know. I am not suddenly going to be a different guy. Last night was fun, but today we have to get down to business. You have your event and your job and I have a life waiting for me back in LA."

A life back in LA. That had to be important, but she wasn't sure how. Or why he was mentioning it now. Except maybe he thought she'd read more into sleeping with him than she had. Maybe that was an occupational hazard for good old ZB. "Of course you do. That doesn't mean you can't be nice to me. I'm not trying to make you stay. I'm asking for some respect, of course, and good old-fashioned manners."

"I'm sorry. I didn't sleep last night," he mumbled.

She walked over to him and had to ball her hands into fists to keep from reaching out and touching him. "I'm sorry. Thank you for thinking of me and leaving when you did. But you could have stayed."

He nodded. "Thanks, babe. But it would have been a complication for both of us."

One he didn't want.

"Fair enough. Is there anything I can do to help you out? You said you have a lot going on and I'm really good at organizing things."

He stood and pulled her into his arms, hugging her close to him. "Don't let me wreck you."

She glanced up at his face, putting her hand on his jaw. "You won't. You're not that kind of man."

He shook his head. "How can you be sure?"

"I'm starting to get to know you. Also you have some really nice friends. Good people here with you."

He swallowed and just nodded. "The team is the best. Let's go and see them."

He took her hand as he led her out of his office and back to the room where Dawn and Vito were, and she noticed that Shantal had joined them. They all started talking to her and Zach, and she got swept into the makeup chair, realizing that he had never really answered any of the questions she'd asked.

She tried not to let that seem important, but she knew it was. He didn't want to wreck her. She knew that there was a side to him she didn't know. *Couldn't* know because this wasn't his world and truly, did she want to be a part of that?

He was helping her grow her online presence and this makeover was something that she knew she'd take with her for the rest of her life. Lila had seen how the right clothes and hairstyle and some subtle makeup could change how she felt about herself. She was curious how everyone on the committee and in the Edmond family would react to her now.

But she was bothered by the way that the more she changed the less Zach interacted with her. He said that he hadn't slept the night before and she knew from experience that she was out of sorts if she didn't get a good night's sleep, but at the same time this felt like something more.

As if the more she changed into someone from his world, the less open he was with her. He'd suggested this makeover but he might not actually like the woman he had helped create.

Did that matter? She had to like this for herself, and she did. She wanted to be the woman she saw in the mirror and not the smart, nerdy girl she'd always been.

Nine

Lila had suggested Sheen for the advisory board meeting because she knew that the added publicity from having Zach tweet about it wouldn't hurt. And Charlotte was her friend and she loved the food there. But now she was second-guessing herself.

Vito and Shantal had come to her place to show her how to get ready with the tools she had. Vito had laughed at the drugstore curling iron she owned and gifted her his Dyson styling tool. Shantal had already given her all the makeup she'd need and now she took her time creating an understated smoky eye.

The Chanel dress that Zach had suggested she wear was a simple black number and she'd paired it with her grandmother's strand of pearls and a Gucci watch that her mom had passed down to her. She had on the Louboutins she'd fallen in love with yesterday. Lila thought she looked both bold and sophisticated in them, but she also couldn't wait to see Zach's reaction to her. When she looked in the mirror she saw the woman she always was in her head, but now the outer packaging matched that inner woman.

She knew she owed that to Zach. He might have helped her out so he didn't have to promote the event on his own, but he'd given her something so much more than she'd anticipated. Who would have thought letting down her guard would net this kind of confidence?

Vito and Shantal had agreed she looked "fabulous" before they left. They'd taken a photo of her putting on her lipstick, and then using the post that Dawn had written for her earlier, she put it on social media. Tagging all the retailers but also #SoireeontheBay.

Lila heard the roar of the Ferrari and then her doorbell rang. Her pulse raced a little bit and she licked her lips at the thought of seeing him again.

She smoothed her hands down the sides of her dress, her hair bouncing around her shoulders in a way it never had before. And when she opened the door, she found Zach standing in front of his car in a navy suit with a white patterned shirt on under it.

He let out a wolf whistle and winked at her.

Zach had been quiet and almost moody when she'd left his house but was more like his regular self now—vivacious and charming. This was the Zach Benning who'd roared into town with a leggy blonde in a vintage Halston dress. It wasn't lost on Lila that she was wearing vintage as she walked down her driveway to get in his car. She saw two of her neighbors out for their nightly walk and waved at them as nonchalantly as she could as Zach held the passenger door open for her.

He waved at them, too.

"You look gorgeous. Sorry if I was an autocrat about the dress," he said. "But damn, babe, you are making me want to take you back inside and skip this dinner."

She arched her eyebrow at him. She wanted that, too. Seeing his reaction had given her a new kind of sexual confidence. "I'd let you, but this meeting is too important to skip. Play your cards right and maybe I'll invite you in later."

"Oh, I'm very good at playing my cards," he rasped, stealing a quick kiss before she seated herself in the car. He closed the door and she put on her seat belt.

"The ladies haven't stopped staring at us since you waved at them."

She blushed. Dammit. When was she going to be able to control that? "It will give them something to talk about at the clubhouse when they take the kids up there to swim."

"Do they gossip about you often?" he asked as he

fired up the powerful engine of the car and drove out of the neighborhood.

"Not usually. But I have heard them gossiping about everything from the other parents in the neighborhood to whatever Mandee Meriweather brings up on *Royal Tonight!*"

"*Royal Tonight!*?"

"It's a local television program, sort of entertainment-news. Mostly gossip about everyone in town. I have been trying to book some time on there to talk about the Soiree on the Bay but she's shut me down so far."

"We'll see what I can do about that," he said, putting his hand on her leg as he drove out of her neighborhood to Sheen.

Sheen had a diverse staff of women who ran everything from the front of house at the restaurant to the kitchen where Charlotte was the head chef. Charlotte worked hand in hand with the staff to ensure it wasn't a gimmicky place. The food was innovative and mouthwatering and its reputation for excellent service was making it "the place" to dine in Royal. Lila was pretty sure the fact that she'd asked Charlotte to book them a table was the only reason they'd gotten one on such short notice.

"I'm not sure where we are going—"

"Lila Jones?"

She turned to see Jack Bowden walking toward her. He was a tall and muscly man who had made his fortune working with his hands. He had an easy smile and normally sort of nodded at her instead of talking to her.

"I thought that was you. You've done something different…with your hair?"

"And a few other things," Zach said, holding out his hand. "I'm Zach Benning, and you are?"

She almost smiled at the way Zach had done that. Was he jealous? She could have told him that Jack wasn't interested in her but was madly in love with Lexi Alderidge. However, the novelty of having anyone jealous over her was interesting.

"Jack Bowden," he said.

"Lila showed me the event grounds that you built. Very impressive," Zach said.

"Is Valencia here yet?" Lila asked.

"I don't think so. But Rusty, Gina and Asher are," Jack said. "Follow me… I'll show you where everyone is."

He turned to lead the way and Zach grabbed her wrist to stop her from going.

"What?" she asked.

"How many men are on this committee?"

"Just Jack and Asher. Ross was but he and his father are having some issues. Then Rusty and Billy are overseeing the event. Why?"

"I just realized I don't know who's on the committee. And the Edmonds?"

"They are royalty right here in Royal. Kind of the money and the brains behind the event. You'll like them, they're your kind of people—movers and shakers."

"Great. Lead on," he said.

She turned to do so and realized, as she walked through the restaurant to the table that had been set aside for them, that for the second time tonight people were watching her.

Lila Jones, nerdy girl next door, was suddenly catching everyone's attention.

She didn't hate it.

The room they were led to was large with a huge chandelier over the long table set for ten. There was a large mirror at the end of the table, and drapes that could be drawn to give them privacy, but Zach noticed they'd left them open while the group was mingling. Which was a great way to get people wondering what they were talking about.

"Let's get a selfie before the meeting starts," he said, putting his arm around her.

"Where should I look?"

"At the camera. Smile and look like you are about to have some fun," he directed.

She made a face, which made him laugh, and he couldn't help it. He hit the shutter button to take a photo. She grimaced. "I looked horrible."

"You looked cute as always. Let's do it for real now," he said, taking a photo.

"Lila, could we see you for a minute?" Jack asked.

She turned to him. "Go ahead," he told her. "I'm

going to post this and go see if I have any followers in the restaurant who will help, as well. I'll be
back in five?"

"That sounds good," she said, moving away from
him toward Jack and the others.

Zach liked the vibe of the restaurant. It was up-
scale but also somehow welcoming. He heard the
entire staff was women and he supported that, but
this felt like more than just some gimmicky one-off.
The dishes both smelled and looked delicious and as
he went to the bar to grab a drink, he was stopped
by a few followers. He took selfies with them and
mentioned Soiree on the Bay.

That's for your conscience, he thought.

He wasn't just using Lila; he was helping her.
And falling for her. It was the combination of heart
and hustle that she brought to everything. The way
that the clothes just made her more Lila instead of
changing her. He hadn't created a safe bridge to cross
when he'd helped her with her makeover; he'd created a woman who was too close to what he hadn't
realized he actually wanted until she'd opened her
door to him and he'd seen her standing there. And
he wanted her more than ever, he thought as he took
a sip of the dry martini he'd ordered. Just what he
needed to get through this meeting. It had been a
long time since he had to socialize like this. Normally everyone was there to see him.

He saw someone walk into the restaurant who

looked familiar. He knew him from somewhere. Maybe LA?

The other man saw him and smiled but didn't seem to recognize him. He continued back to the private room where Zach had left Lila. Zach tipped the bartender and then went back to the group. They were starting to settle into their seats and he noticed that Lila had saved him a seat next to her as the waitstaff drew the curtains around them to afford them privacy.

Once the appetizers had been served and drink orders taken, Rusty Edmond, who was the patriarch of his family, stood up. Everyone immediately stopped talking.

"Thanks to everyone for your hard work. I think we should start with a toast to Jack for all the hard work he put in. The event site is great."

Everyone toasted Jack, who looked humble as he swallowed his drink.

"Lila, darling, do you want to introduce Zach?" Rusty asked.

"Yes, sir. This is Zach Benning. I'm sure y'all have heard of him. He's been tagging the Soiree on his social media accounts and it is working to get the word out. He's also helped me to figure out how to add some pizzazz to our posts."

"Welcome, Zach," everyone said.

Zach nodded. "It's nothing, I'm happy to help out. I do have a few questions about the event, however."

"We will be happy to answer them after the dinner," Rusty said. "Do you know everyone here?"

"Um. Well, I met Jack on the way in," he answered.

"That's my daughter, Gina, stepson Asher. This here is Billy Holmes. Family friend. Valencia is on the end and next to her is Charlotte."

"Billy, have we met before?" Zach asked. The other man looked very familiar.

"I don't think so," he said. "Unless you went to college in Texas?"

"Uh, no. UCLA for me," Zach murmured. "You sure do look familiar."

Billy laughed and nodded at him. "I have one of those faces. Everyone thinks they know me."

"Everyone thinks they know Zach, too," Lila said. "I mean his followers are always swarming around him."

"Are they?" Charlotte asked. "Do you think you could get them to swarm here?"

Charlotte Jarrett was smart, sassy and a great dinner companion. She was the head chef here at Sheen and told him she had a son named Ben who was two. She was engaged to Ross Edmond, who wasn't at the dinner because his father had disinherited him. Sounded like there was more to that story, but Zach didn't ask.

"You don't need my help. This place is packed," he said.

"Yeah, but having a line out the door never hurt a restaurant," she countered.

"I have a few ideas. I already tagged the restaurant and took some selfies with your customers. That should help get the word going," he said.

"Thanks. Now about Lila…"

"What about her?" Zach asked.

"I saw you blaze into town with that blonde and now, what, less than a week later you're here with her? Lila's a friend and I don't want to see her get hurt," Charlotte said.

"I don't, either," Zach promised. "I'm just helping her learn how to promote the Soiree without me. She needs to be able to do this on her own."

"It looks like it's more than that."

"She's a grown woman," Zach reminded her.

Charlotte narrowed her eyes at him. "All right. Just don't come back around here if you hurt her."

Valencia asked her a question and she turned to answer it. Zach was left in the middle of one of those dinner party silences where the people on either side of him were engaged in other conversation. He heard Billy laugh and shook his head. He was sure he'd met the other man somewhere. It would come to him eventually.

He looked over at Lila, who was in her element, talking about the town and the upcoming event, and he knew that Charlotte was right. He couldn't hurt her. She wasn't used to his life, and he might have changed the outer packaging, but he didn't want to change anything else.

"I love those shoes," Gina raved as they were all standing in the bathroom fixing their lipstick after dinner.

"Thanks. I thought they'd be uncomfortable, but

they aren't," Lila said. For the first time in her life, she'd gone to the ladies' room with the other women at her table. She never had a reason to freshen up after dinner as she usually didn't care if her lipstick had worn off.

Charlotte had dashed to the kitchen to check on her sous-chef and make sure that everything was running smoothly. Valencia finished touching up her lipstick and they ran into Charlotte as they walked out. Lila knew this would be a perfect photo for her to post.

"Ladies, do you mind taking a selfie? Maybe with the Sheen logo behind us?" Lila asked.

They seemed surprised that she was suggesting a selfie, but all were game. Lila realized her arms were too short to get a good photo but Valencia offered to hold the camera and they got one of them all. She followed the women back toward their private table, remembering the tips that Dawn had given her for posting. She was toying with some different hashtags when Mandee Meriweather stopped her.

"Lila Jones, you are all that everyone is talking about tonight…well, you and Zach Benning. His Benningnites have been bombarding me, demanding I interview him. I'd love to have you both on the show. What do you say?" she asked.

"Oh, Mandee, thanks. I have been wanting to come on and talk about the Soiree," Lila said. "Let me talk to ZB and I'll let you know when we can do it."

"Oh, ZB…so are you part of his inner circle?" Mandee asked.

Lila knew that Mandee was absolutely the biggest gossip in town—Lila's dad referred to her as the Mouth of the South. No doubt, she'd love to get the inside scoop on what Zach was doing here.

"We're friends," she said. "I'll message you a time that works."

She smiled her goodbye before she turned and walked away from the woman who'd been ignoring her requests for months. It felt good to be the one in this position. Lila had never experienced this before. But she knew she had something that Mandee wanted. For once, the other woman had to come to her.

She finished writing her post but didn't post it; she wanted to get Zach's feedback first. He came over to her when she entered the private dining area.

"Everything okay?"

"Yes. *Royal Tonight!* wants to interview us. Probably just you but she wasn't about to say that to my face. I told her we'd get back to her on a time. Can you look at this? I want to post it."

She handed him her phone and he scanned it, added a hashtag and then nodded. "Looks great."

She glanced down at the hashtag he'd added— #soireefoxyfour. "What if the other women don't want—"

"It's fun and it brands you four. I think it will work. If you want to get their approval first, then let's ask them."

He put his hand on the small of her back and took

her over to the rest of the group. Everyone stopped talking when they joined them. "What do you think of the ladies being branded as the Soiree Foxy Four? Just a fun hashtag that the team can use when they post?" he asked.

"I think it might be a bit much for Royal, and the Soiree *is* a charity event," Gina said.

"I agree," Valencia said. "But thanks for thinking of us as the foxy four."

Lila deleted the hashtag and then sent the post as Asher came over to talk to them.

"Zach, I like your thinking. You are just what this event needs," he said.

"You were already in good hands with this advisory committee. I'm impressed with everything you have brought to the table."

"Yeah? It's fun to see something go from concept to reality," Asher said.

"It is," Lila agreed. "I can't believe we are only two months away. Zach, you came at exactly the right time."

"Well, if I'd known how charming Royal was, I would have been here sooner," he admitted.

Zach glanced at his watch and she wondered if he was ready to leave. Normally she would have lit out after dessert but here she was staying for drinks with the group. As much as she enjoyed it she wouldn't mind some quiet time with Zach. A lot had happened today, and she still wasn't sure where they stood.

But she was going to be chill. She'd made up her mind sometime during the afternoon when Shantal was showing her how to do a cat-eye with eyeliner. She couldn't be that small-town girl who clung to the bad boy. But the problem was she wanted more from Zach. More of what she didn't know. But definitely more.

"Where is Billy from? He looks so familiar to me," Zach said.

Lila shrugged. She didn't know his history. "He doesn't remember meeting you and I'm pretty sure if you had met that wouldn't be the case."

"Why is that?" he asked, pulling her closer to him.

"You're unforgettable, ZB," she said, forcing herself to be flirty, but inside she knew she meant those words. That they were a truth bomb that she should pay attention to. No matter what happened between them, she knew she'd never forget him. How could she?

He'd changed something in her, helped her see her life in a new light and sparked her desires for something that she'd never considered before. That this craving for a lifestyle that she'd never dreamed possible could be so tantalizing and fun with the right man by her side. She wanted to say he'd given her a glimpse of life beyond what she'd had but honestly, he'd made her realize how much she loved her city and her life here, and that maybe she wanted him to love it, too.

Ten

Zach dropped Lila off at her house after their dinner at Sheen. She was getting a bunch of likes from being featured on his social media account and he was getting DMs asking if she was his flavor of the week. He had to think about that, and not with Lila.

"Are you sure you won't come in?" she asked.

She was breathtakingly gorgeous, and he wanted nothing more than to come in and hook up with her again. But that wasn't going to help either of them. Either she was his pet project or she was his girlfriend. But she couldn't be both, and a part of him was beginning to realize no matter how he spun it, there was no way to keep people from seeing her as his latest arm candy.

"I don't think that's a good idea," he said.

"Why not?" she asked, quirking her head to the side, but keeping her expression blank.

"Just for once don't ask the questions I'm not sure I can answer," he bit out.

"Why can't you answer that?" she asked.

It was almost ten o'clock and her neighborhood was quiet. Everyone in their homes watching TV or sleeping. Just a quiet domestic scene that was as foreign to him as tagging a post had been to Lila. This was her world.

Zach wanted to repeat it to himself, but he knew he wasn't stupid and he already got it. He didn't fit in here. Part of him didn't *want* to. The only thing he wanted was Lila… What if he took her to his place? Enough of this sleepy little suburban neighborhood.

"Want to come and stay with me?"

"No. You have your team there and they already think we are sleeping together," she said. "Come inside so we can talk. I can see one of my neighbors pretending not to stare at us."

"Fine. But we are already sleeping together," he reminded her as he turned off the Ferrari and followed her into her house.

As soon as the door closed behind him she turned to him. "I know that. But I don't want them to know."

"You should know everyone who has liked our posts where I tagged you also thinks we are sleeping together."

"Ugh! I need a drink."

She tossed her purse on the antique table in the hall and walked toward her kitchen. He put his keys on the table and followed her. Lila had pushed a chair over to the fridge, kicking off her Louboutin pumps, before he realized what she was doing. She started to climb up on it, but he caught her by her waist and set her aside.

"I'll get whatever it is you are trying to reach," he said, pushing the chair aside and opening the cabinet. There was an unopened bottle of bourbon, a partially drunk bottle of Jack Daniel's and two bottles of Casamigos tequila. One of them was almost empty and the other hadn't been opened.

"Tequila?"

"Yes," she said stiffly. She had moved to another cabinet and taken two lowball glasses from it. Then she used her hand to get ice from the ice maker and dropped two cubes in one of the glasses. "Do you want ice?"

"Yes, ma'am," he said. He wasn't 100 percent sure what had set her off but he guessed learning that most of his million followers had figured out they were doing the horizontal mambo was it.

"Lime?"

"Please."

She opened the fridge and he poured them both a few fingers of tequila. Then she squeezed a lime wedge over one of them and handed him the other one. She lifted the glass and took a hard swallow. Then she put the glass down.

She nodded a bunch of times and put her hands on her hips. "Okay. I got this. We are sleeping together, and everyone knows… It's the twenty-first century, so who cares?"

She did. It was very obvious to him that Lila Jones didn't like anyone to know her personal business. He hated to see her like this. This was what he'd wanted to avoid. He hadn't expected this to bother her as much as it did because she was so open about other things—hell, pretty much everything else.

"*You* do," he said gently. "I should have warned you. But to be honest, even if we hadn't slept together, people would still think we had. You know my reputation."

"I do. But you're not—hell, yes you are. You are as tempting as everyone thinks you are… I don't want to be your flavor of the week," she said. "There, I said it. I don't need promises of forever, but I don't want to be someone you forget as soon as you drive out of town in your fast car, either."

He looked over at her and knew that she needed something from him. Something real. Not a glib statement or another diversion. "I could never forget you, Lila."

She shook her head and took another healthy swallow of her tequila. "I bet you even said that to that blonde who was with you when you got to town—oh, my God, that was only a few days ago!"

She was losing herself in this spiral.

He removed the glass from her hand before she

had another sip and took her hand in his, drawing her back into the hallway and down to the mirror that hung there. He turned her to face it and stepped behind her, putting one arm around her waist.

"Lila Jones, look at yourself in the mirror," he said.

"I'm the woman you made me," she whispered.

He kissed her temple. "I wish I could make someone as strong, smart and sophisticated as you are. I did nothing but help you find a way to wear well-made clothes and get other people to notice that. There is nothing about you that wasn't already there."

She leaned closer to stare at herself and he waited. He felt her settling down, but he knew she needed more from him. Something *real*. Not the facade that ZB provided to his online followers but something authentic that Zach could give to Lila. He wanted to just do it, but deep down he was afraid. Afraid to lower his guard and let her see that he wasn't all shiny and perfect away from his online accounts.

"Everyone believes what they will because of me. But anyone who has met you will probably come to the same conclusion that I have."

"What is that?" she asked, turning her head slightly to meet his gaze over her shoulder.

That she was too damned good for him. That if anyone was the flavor of the week it was him and not her.

"That we are one hell of a pair," he said. Chickening out because the truth wasn't going to do anything but leave him weak to her.

Lila felt so unsure of herself and this wasn't like her. She turned in Zach's arms and hugged him. He hugged her back and she knew she'd probably freaked him out. She hadn't meant to. It was just that tonight had been filled with so many highs and the adrenaline rush had been exhilarating.

And then…she'd started to let doubts creep in. Did she only belong because of him? Zach had the contacts and the pizzazz that they needed, and sure, he was showing her how to bring that limelight to herself and the Soiree, but she wasn't going to kid herself that she was really part of that world. She liked the way she looked and how it felt to have everyone's attention, but there was another part of her that wasn't too sure she'd want it forever.

"Brown Eyes, please don't be sad. I can't do sad," he said as he tipped her head back.

Brown Eyes.

That was the first nickname he'd used that she actually didn't mind. She smiled at him. "I won't. Sorry for that. I am pretty sure this is the only time my personal life has been interesting."

"It's not boring to me," he said.

She tried not to let it matter that he had once again turned the conversation to himself. But Zach lived his life in front of the camera. Living the scandals and gossip-worthy life 24/7. "You were never like this?"

She gestured to her normal house, and herself, really hoping he'd understand she meant her normal life.

"No. I mean this house is really nice, but I have never lived in someplace as quaint as this one," he said. "I kind of like this. It's so homey and comfortable. I feel like…well, like I can just let my guard down while I'm here."

She snapped her fingers. "You know what I could do?"

"What?" he asked, sounding a bit wary.

"I could show you this life. Show you how to chill and not post every detail of your life. That way…it would be more even."

He stared down at her as if she'd grown a second head and she held her breath. She needed this and she wasn't sure how she'd missed it before. But her relationship with Zach was always going to be lopsided until she could give him something he couldn't buy for himself.

"I'm not sure…why wouldn't I post it all?"

"Just try it. Put your phone away for the rest of the night. And hang with me. Just doing fun stuff."

"Sex?" he asked. "I wouldn't need my phone for that."

Sex. Sure, she wanted him again. She doubted that she was ever going to tire of having him in her bed and ravishing her body. But she wanted something else. "Yes, but more than that. How about you park your car in my garage and we chill out. Doing the kinds of things that everyone does but no one posts."

"I can't even fathom what that would be."

"Watching TV, reading, playing spit."

"Okay, I'm intrigued. What the heck is spit?"

"Park your car and I'll show you."

She wasn't sure he'd do it. As much as she'd freaked out and drunk tequila, he seemed a bit like he was unsure, as well. But he just nodded and went to move his car. She opened the garage for him and then waited. Twenty minutes later they were both dressed in un-post-worthy clothes—Zach in his gym clothes, Lila in a pair of Looney Tunes boxers and an oversize tee—eating popcorn she'd topped with Parmesan cheese and butter, and she was giving him an overview of playing spit.

"We don't take turns but both play at the same time. Since it's your first time when we are ready to begin you can say spit. Then we will both start placing our cards down. You can only put a card on top that is either one higher or lower than the card showing."

"Okay, I think I got that. Can we play on each other's cards? How does one of us win?"

"Yes, we can. We keep going until one of us runs out of cards. If we get blocked then one of us says *ready spit* and we get sort of a free card," she said. "Ready?"

"Spit!"

They played for thirty minutes and she soon realized that Zach wasn't paying attention to the cards at all but watching her.

"Do you like playing cards?"

"I like poker, but that is about it. Nothing this exciting."

"You are totally teasing me," she said.

"I am. But I love how excited you are," he admitted gruffly. "It turns me on."

"*You* turn me on. You aren't even trying to win," she pointed out after he missed two obvious plays.

"My mom taught me it wasn't polite to beat a lady at games," he said. "Especially a lady you want to take home."

He had his own version of manners. "What else did your mom teach you?"

Lila knew his father had cheated and that he'd grown up with his mom. She could have googled him and found out more about his past but when she'd been researching Zach that hadn't mattered. All that mattered at the time were his followers. But now... well, now she wanted to hear his story from him and not read it on the internet.

"The usual stuff," he said. "How to throw a great party. You have to have the right mix of people. Talkers, listeners, shit stirrers and peacemakers."

"Huh, I never thought of it that way, but you are right. That's a good mix. Which one are you?"

"I can be all of them depending on the party." He grinned. "Like right now, I'm listening."

"You were. Now I am."

"Yes. Everything is give-and-take. Not like you said earlier. I'd never just let you use me."

"You wouldn't?" she asked, finally getting to the heart of what was bothering her.

"No."

"So what are you getting?"

"You," he said, pushing himself up on his hands and knees and kissing her.

Zach hadn't meant for this to happen. But somehow, he felt even more vulnerable to her as she sat across from him playing this card game that made no sense and had no reason to it. He was also getting more and more aroused as she continued to play cards, point out ones he'd missed and generally just let her guard down.

Until this moment he hadn't realized how much of herself she kept locked away. But now he knew. She'd let him in a few times before, and then tonight when she'd been afraid that everything about him was just for show, she'd kind of lost it. But him sitting here with her had somehow reassured her.

Which he wouldn't allow himself to analyze. He'd been staring at her breasts under that large T-shirt since she'd sat down next to him. They were under the fan and he could tell the exact moment when she'd gotten cold. Her nipples had hardened and then *he'd* hardened.

Her mouth under his was soft but the angle was

wrong, so he pulled her into his arms and rolled until they were both on their sides staring into each other's eyes. She put one hand on his hip and the other on his chest. Her breath smelled of lime and tequila and it wasn't unpleasant, but it served to remind him of how fragile she was right now.

Zach hugged her close because he had no idea what to do next. He could take what he wanted—her body. He could turn her on enough that she'd stop worrying about the fact that everyone knew they were sleeping together.

"What am I going to do with you, Brown Eyes?"

She tipped her head back, lightly bumping his chin as she did so. "Make love to me."

Make love.

Those were words he never applied to sex. He called it everything but that because love…well, he knew it didn't really exist. That it was as hollow as the likes he racked up with each new post, yet at the same time…tonight he wished he could make love to her.

He swiftly took her clothes off and then stripped his off, as well. Before he realized he'd left his condoms in her bedroom.

"Be right back."

He hurried and got one. When he returned, she was lying in the middle of the blanket where they'd been playing cards, propped up on her elbow, her hair falling around her shoulders.

"Hey there," she said.

Something emotional surged to life within him and he quickly quelled it. Shoved it deep down inside so he didn't have to acknowledge it. Instead, he got down on his hands and knees and crawled to her feet. He kissed her delicate ankle and then slowly worked his way up her body, pushing her onto her back when he reached the apex of her thighs. He moved between them and lowered his head. Tasting her first with his tongue in slow licks and then as she started to move under him, her hips undulating with each probe of his tongue, he sucked her clit into his mouth. She grabbed the back of his head, holding him to her while she pushed herself up against him.

He reached up with one hand, finding her hard nipple with his fingers and pinching it as he continued to eat her. She pulled on his head and he lifted himself up, looking up her flushed body.

"Take me now," she said. "I need you."

He slid up her body and shifted his hips until he was poised at her entrance, then drove himself deep inside her. As that tightness inside him started to unravel with each thrust, he pounded into her again and again until he felt the skin at the back of his neck tingle and his balls felt full and tight. Then he came, thrusting into her a few more times as she tightened around his shaft and called out his name.

He kept moving until he was fully drained and then collapsed on her, careful to use his legs and his arms to keep from crushing her. He rolled to his side, pulling her with him and holding her cradled against his side. She put her hand on his chest right over his heart and did that thing with her fingertip she'd done before.

She looked up at him.

"I guess they are all right."

"They?"

"Your followers who think we are sleeping together," she said.

"Does that matter?" he asked. He wished he could say the words that would make this easy for her. But they would be a lie, and he had never lied to anyone. He might be a bad boy, but he'd never been a bad man. He sort of prided himself on that.

"I don't think it does. I would rather be in your arms than not because I was being spiteful."

He smiled down at her. "Spiteful to who?"

"I guess myself. I don't know where this is going, Zach, and I might have regrets later. But for now, I'm going to enjoy being with you."

They weren't words he wanted to hear but he'd heard them before. He was the kind of man who knew his place in a woman's life, and it was temporary. No matter how much he might wish that it could be different.

Eleven

Lila was amazed the next day at work by the number of calls she got about the Soiree by the Bay. Not only that but her social media posts were racking up likes—the ones *she* posted, not just the ones that Zach tagged her in. She knew a big part of that was due to the fact that many people thought they were a couple.

Of course, they were a couple, but she also cautioned herself not to buy into the show. Zach traveled with a team and everything he did was for his followers. He had invited her to join him for lunch and taken her on a helicopter ride to a field of bluebonnets. And when they got there Shantal, Vito and Dawn were waiting with Mrs. Smith and several cameras. So the romantic lunch she'd thought she was having was actually a business lunch.

She knew that she had to start thinking that way. Like tonight when they went on Mandee's show, she had to be ready. Zach had texted her that he was coming by her office to introduce her to a media expert who would prep her for being on television.

Lila found herself pulling out her makeup and touching it up before he arrived. Her phone vibrated on her desk, but she was getting so many notifications now that she didn't even bother checking it. Probably more likes.

What a difference a few days made! She used to have seven likes—*seven*—but on her posts now she had thousands.

"Hello, babe," Zach said as he breezed into her office, accompanied by a beautiful woman who was immaculately dressed in a black business jacket over a button-down shirt and a pair of loose-fitting jeans.

She was beginning to read his signs. He called her *babe* when he was working. When they were alone… *Brown Eyes*. So this was a business call, which she'd known.

"Hey, ZB."

"This is Bree, the media expert I told you about."

"Hello," Lila said.

"Hi there. I have been checking out your social media feed and you seem pretty savvy so I'm not sure how much I can help," Bree said as she and Zach took seats in the guest chairs in her office.

"That's all ZB and his team's advice," Lila said. "I've only been on TV once before."

"Really?" Zach asked, giving her a quizzical look. "I didn't know that."

"Well, it was when I went to Congrès in high school and got first in the dictation contest. It's a French-speaking competition."

"Wow, I had no idea you *parles français*," Zach said.

"That's because I don't anymore. I mean I might be able to conjugate a few verbs for you but that's about it."

He laughed.

"Don't worry about your lack of TV presence," Bree told her. "The important thing is to be prepared and to remember your message. ZB already filled me in on the Soiree but he didn't need to. I've been hearing about it all over the state. It is going to be *the* event of the summer season."

"Thanks. We have all been working so hard and I'm excited to see it come together. So my message should be about the event. Just facts?" she asked.

"Facts, yes, but also why no one should miss the event," Bree said. "Who is performing there?"

"We have Kingston Blue lined up. He's so hot right now. I think just saying his name will get everyone excited," Lila said. The musician had been one of the first to respond to the event—he was tall, with gorgeous dreadlocks down over his shoulders, and a flashy dresser.

"Okay, so instead of just saying we've booked Kingston Blue, lead in with the 'Song of Summer,' Kingston's latest hit, and say you've had it on repeat on your playlist. Something along those lines," Bree suggested.

"I can do that," Lila said. "And it's not a lie. I mean that song is as hot as summer in Texas. So sensual and sexy. Should I do that with everyone?"

"Well, don't do the same thing each time. Just look at the facts you want to get out. Booking tickets and promoting the website…don't need an anecdote but maybe a few festival stories or something. And Zach will be there with you. How well do you two know each other?" she asked.

"Uh…" Lila began.

"I know the gossip, but that's all publicity. What I'm trying to say here is that if you know each other well then Zach can lead you to the topics," Bree said, turning to look at him. "My man ZB is an expert at directing the conversation where he wants it to go."

Lila let out a breath she hadn't realized she'd been holding. She hadn't expected that there would be people who would just dismiss the gossip about the two of them. But she should have. It made her feel better to know that most people weren't going to be thinking of them doing the nasty each time Zach tagged her in a photo.

"I do. And I'm going to be pretty strict about not talking about Candi. I think I already mentioned that to Mandee's people. We are on the show to discuss the Soiree and of course all things fab."

She smiled, but she knew him well enough now to hear the edge in his voice. Zach wasn't prepared to discuss his affair with a married woman. He hadn't mentioned it to her, either, and she honestly wasn't too sure she wanted the details. But she did wonder how he was going to keep Mandee from asking about it. She was known for getting the dirt she wanted.

Bree left her with a few more tips and Lila told her she would do her best to implement them. Zach closed the door behind Bree and then turned to face her.

"Ready for this?"

"No. I'm so nervous, but I will give it my all."

"I know you will," he said. "I don't want any of the scandal from my life to touch you. I'm going to let you take point on the interview. Just be your besotted boyfriend."

"Is that what you are?"

He had no idea. The longer Zach was in Royal and with Lila, the less clear a lot of things were. Even his online life had started to take a back seat to this time he was spending with her. He'd been trying to stay focused and ignore the emotions that Lila stirred in him and so far he'd been shooting above par. Which wasn't good. He wanted to at least be on par.

"Isn't that what you want me to be?" he asked, pulling her into his arms because he'd been wanting to kiss her since he'd walked into her office. Her new glasses suited her face and when he'd entered and seen her sitting there, he had a few racy fantasies involving her and that desk of hers.

She put her hand on his chest to keep some distance between the two of them. "Don't be glib. I want to know how you see yourself."

Glib. That was his life. It was how he managed everything and normally no one dared to call him on it, but he might have let Lila get too close. He wasn't even sure how he'd done that. After all, he'd been making *her* over, dammit. But at the same time, without him being aware, she might have made a few changes in him. Because he knew he didn't want to hurt her feelings. Didn't want to say something that was going to make those big brown eyes of hers regard him the way so many disappointed people had.

"Brown Eyes, please. I'm doing my best here."

"I'm not sure that you are," she said. "I'm going to be honest and lay it all on the line, Zach. I'm not an influencer, and those pictures I post? Well, as much as I'm following the tips that Dawn gave me, they are my life. I'm not tagging you to get followers but because I like the pictures of the two of us. And before you say anything, I do know that it's for show. In my mind, I know that. But I'm also starting to buy it. To buy *us*."

Zach took a deep breath. Was that it? Were they both starting to buy into the image they created to build her followers? Was he falling for the ruse the same way that she was? This was fun. But he knew that if he said that to her right now, she wouldn't appreciate that.

"I don't know what to say. This is so not my normal scene. Royal is different. *You* are different. Maybe… I have to be back in LA soon. Why don't you come with me?" he asked.

She turned out of his arms and walked around behind her desk, sitting down. She was thinking about his offer. He remembered how the blonde— he couldn't even remember her name now—had just jumped in his car when he'd asked her to come with him to Texas. But Lila didn't make decisions that way.

Zach leaned against the wall. He could only imagine what she was thinking, probably running the pros and cons of the trip.

"It will be a lot of fun and I'll introduce you to more people who you can invite to the Soiree. The kind of people you need to get on board if you want this to be a big international event."

"Are you bribing me?" she asked.

He held his hands out to his sides. "I'll do whatever it takes to get you to come to my home with me."

"Just ask me," she said.

That honesty.

Damn.

She killed him with that. *Just ask her.* Well, now he couldn't because he knew if he did, she'd know he wanted her there. *Yo, idiot, she knows.* His sub-conscious was giving him a hard time lately.

"Come home with me," he said, forcing the words out as fast as he could.

"Okay."

What?

That was it?

"Seriously, that's all you needed to give up your lists?"

She shook her head and smiled at him. "How do you know I was making a mental list?"

"It's you. That's what you do."

She stood up and came around the desk, leaning back against it as she looked over at him. "You're starting to know me."

"I am," he admitted thickly. Which was why he had to get them back to LA. Back to the place where the world made sense and he could forget about these feelings that were stirring inside him.

"So we can leave tomorrow… Do you have to clear it with someone here?"

She groaned. "I do. In fact, you should leave because I have to do some work before the interview, and I want to try to get an appointment with Abby Carmichael. Do you know her?"

"Uh, no. Serious documentary filmmakers don't dig my scene," he said. But he'd heard of her and knew she'd do a great job when Lila convinced her to come and film the event.

He knew Lila would get Abby on board, too. She

was good at getting people to do what she wanted. He left her office and went to the coffee shop across the street but was mobbed by his followers and left after agreeing to a few selfies. Then he found himself driving away from Royal until there was nothing but flat Texas landscape on either side of the road.

He pulled over.

Had Lila been manipulating him? He had to wonder about that because he wasn't acting like himself. It was easy to say she was making him feel things. Really, he had to figure out his emotions and stop referring to them as something he couldn't define. But this was the first time he'd experienced them.

And it was down to her.

Was that part of her plan?

Hell. He didn't know or care. He liked her. He liked the time he spent with her. He knew it would end; everything did. So he was going to enjoy the ride for as long as he could. He knew that once she saw him in LA her opinion of him would change. She'd fall in love with the lifestyle and forget all about the man who had introduced her to it.

Mandee Meriweather was very attractive and sort of made for the spotlight. Lila was in the greenroom by herself waiting for the show to start. Zach had texted he was on his way.

"Oh, all alone?" Mandee asked. She wore a black sheath sundress with large straps that left her shoulders and neck bare. She was followed by a cloud of Chanel No. 5 as she entered the greenroom and looked around expectantly.

"ZB is on his way. And his team are looking for a parking spot."

"Sorry about that. I didn't know there would be so many different vehicles. So exciting about the Soiree. I know that you have been on the planning committee from the beginning. Quite the coup for you. Little, shy Lila Jones."

She'd known Mandee in high school…well, more like known *of* her in high school, as the other woman was popular and had run with a different crowd.

"I don't think it was anything like that. I mean it is my job to promote Royal at the chamber of commerce."

"Of course it is, silly. So when did you say Zach would be here?"

"Now," he said, walking in and coming straight over to Lila and giving her a one-armed hug. "Sorry for being late."

"That's okay," she murmured, glad that he was here. Mandee was the kind of person that Zach was an expert at dealing with.

"Mandee, you look gorg tonight," he declared, turning to her.

"Thanks, ZB—is it okay to call you that?"

"Only my closest pals do," he said, flirting with her. "So of course you can."

"Ooooh, thanks for that. How about a selfie before the show?" she asked.

Lila was trying not to be jealous of the way Zach was flirting with Mandee. A part of her knew it was just the way the two of them interacted, but at the same time, Lila couldn't help thinking that the flamboyant reporter was more the kind of woman that Zach was used to.

"The Benningnites will love seeing me with you two," Zach said, pulling Lila along with him.

Mandee got in close on his other side. "Maybe it would be better if Lila snapped the pic?"

Lila smiled to herself. "It would be. You two get close."

She had to give it to Zach—he looked like he was really interested in being photographed with Mandee, and she knew that was part of his charm. He loved this life. It wasn't something he was doing for a lark. As he chatted with Mandee and his team arrived to touch up her makeup and do some final details on Zach's hair, she saw him sort of getting even more electric. Everyone in the room wanted to talk to him and be near him.

He had a real gift. She might think this was all an illusion, and for her, she reminded herself, it was. But for him this was *real*.

Mandee had to leave to go and prep for their segment, and the team departed along with her. When a production assistant came to get her and Zach a few minutes later, Lila realized her hands were sweating.

She wiped them on her hips and he caught the movement. "Don't worry. You're going to be great.

Just remember to smile, to breathe and that I'm right by your side."

Impulsively she hugged him. "Thank you."

"It's nothing."

But it wasn't nothing, she thought as she sat next to him on Mandee's guest couch to talk about the Soiree. She got in the information she'd practiced with Bree and a few other facts, as well. The crew for the show all responded to her stories so she thought that went well.

"So word on the street is that you two are Royal's hottest new couple," Mandee said.

"Lila is a gem," Zach replied, flashing his trademark grin. "I came to town because of the event and that is down to the hard work of the committee, but especially Lila. She has a way of making Royal seem like the only place I want to be."

"We are pretty special here."

"Yes, but it's also Lila herself. She's got the kind of Southern charm that I've always heard about but found in short supply," he said, reaching over to take her hand in his and lifting it to his mouth to kiss the back of it. "It's easy to fall for her appeal."

Fall for…

Her heart stuttered in her chest. Was Zach telling her how he felt? It would be just like him to do it in the spotlight, but at the same time, the Zach she knew was very private. This had to be for show. To keep the numbers of her followers up because she appeared to be special to him. That was all it was.

She had to be very careful not to fall for this silver-tongued rascal. He was merely doing the job she'd asked him to do.

"Of course, ZB's pretty special, too. I can't wait for everyone to meet him at the Soiree on the Bay," Lila said, trying to bring the conversation back to the event and to force herself to remember that was the real reason he was here.

"It will be one hot July on the bay," Zach declared. "And I can't wait."

"I think we all want to be there," Mandee said. "Ticket and festival information is available at the website shown on the screen right now, and make sure to follow Lila Jones and ZB on all social media platforms for behind-the-scenes deets. Until next time, this has been *Royal Tonight!*"

The closing music played and they all stayed seated and smiling until the stage manager called cut.

"Thanks for having us on your show," Lila said.

"It was a blast," Zach added.

"I hope you will come back again closer to the event," Mandee said. "Want to grab a drink?"

"Love to, but can't," Zach replied. "We are heading to LA in the morning and I promised Lila we'd have a quiet night."

"Lucky girl," Mandee said.

Zach slipped his hand into hers again and now she wasn't sure if this was all for show or for real. She knew that she needed to figure it out, however, because she was starting to fall for him.

Twelve

"Welcome to my home," Zach said as he swept into the large foyer of a huge mansion in Beverly Hills. "I am throwing a party in Malibu in a couple of days, but for today it's just us. I want you to have a chance to get used to the time change and all that."

Lila stood next to him, her Birkin bag over her shoulder, just turning slowly in a circle and taking in the entryway of his house. The marble flooring was Carrara and had been flown in from Italy. And the art on the walls were some of his favorite modern artists, including a print on canvas of Edvard Munch's *Vampire*, or as it was originally titled, *Love and Pain*. It was a conversation starter when people came to his home.

For the first time he saw the image through different eyes. He had hesitated to say he was in love, but seeing the couple bound together in the image made him think of himself and Lila.

"I'm not sure about this painting. It's so dark but also so sensual," Lila said when she came to a stop in front of it.

"That's why I picked it," he said, coming next to her and returning his attention to the portrait of the couple. The man had his head in the lap of the woman as she cradled him. He knew from his study of the artist that Munch had been dealing with his own psychological issues, but this portrait had spoken to him.

Next to it was one of his favorite pieces—a bright neon sign that spelled out *You Wish You Were Me!*

"Nice. I guess it takes a humble man to hang that up."

"It was a gag gift from a friend. It makes me laugh and not take myself too seriously." Zach knew that he could come off as totally self-centered, but he also didn't really take himself too seriously. He wanted the chance to show Lila his world. To see if what he felt for her was just a Royal thing or if those feelings were something different, something deeper and more intense than he wanted to admit.

They stowed her bags in the master bedroom. "Are you tired or do you want to go sightseeing?"

"I don't know! I've never been to California before. Did you grow up here?"

"I did. In Bel Air. It's not too far from here," he said. Thinking of his childhood always stirred bittersweet memories. His younger self hadn't realized everything wasn't about him, and it wasn't until it was too late that he cottoned on to the reality of his parents' marriage.

"Oh, do you want to show me your childhood home? I like that idea. And then you can take me somewhere super posh for lunch and we can try shopping again," she said.

"I've created a monster," he joked. His childhood home wasn't a place he went to often and it was odd that he had brought it up now. But there was something about Lila that made him feel and remember things that he'd ignored for too long.

"Ha. You wish," she said. "Should I change?"

"Yes. Put on that cute BCBG Max Azria outfit you modeled for me," he suggested. "It shows off your arms and makes your legs look a mile long."

"Oh, I will."

She dashed into the bathroom and got changed while he waited. Normally he would be on the phone going live for his followers trying to drum up a crowd to follow him that day, but he realized he wanted this first day in LA with Lila just for himself. He loved her excitement and wonder when she experienced something new and couldn't wait to see her face when they drove past the Hollywood sign. He knew she'd love it.

She liked all those things that people were jaded

about out here. Lila got riveted by a pretty sunset or the way the bluebonnets smelled. She was just so genuine in liking the little things and well, let's be honest, the expensive things, too. But he wanted this day for them.

And he knew why. He wanted to see if the hollow aching part inside him would be satisfied with just Lila. This trip wasn't just to see if his feelings were real outside of Texas, they were to see if Lila fit in here, too. He wasn't sure if he wanted her to. If she did, how was he going to deal with that? He was so used to hiding his emotions behind the flashy lifestyle. If he had someone to share it with—if he shared it with *Lila*—he'd have to be real all the time. He'd never been able to quiet that need to find the spotlight and draw strangers to him, but with Lila he suspected he had a chance.

"How do I look?"

Drop-dead gorgeous. She had on a sleeveless knit top that came to a deep vee over her breasts and a pair of wide-legged trousers and some wedge sandals that made her seem even taller than normal. She'd pulled her hair back at the sides and her old fall of bangs were back. He hadn't realized how much he'd missed the woman he'd first met until now.

"Fab. Ready to take LA?"

"With you by my side? Always."

She pulled out some large shades from her Birkin and put them on before looping her arm through his. He walked her to the garage and she pulled her sunglasses off as the motion sensor lights slowly came on, illuminating the five cars he kept there. She pulled her arm from his and turned to him.

"I can't believe this! My dad would go nuts for that '69 Camaro."

"Give me your phone and we can send him a photo of you with it," he said. "Is that the car you want to take?"

She didn't even bother looking at the rest of the vehicles in the garage, just nodded. "Oh, yeah."

He snapped her photos in front of the white car that had been lovingly restored with the bright orange racing stripe down the center of it. Then he put the ragtop down on the convertible before he fired up the V8 engine. He seldom drove the classic muscle car because his followers preferred the newer Audi or Aston Martin, but for Lila he'd drive this.

It wasn't until they had driven past his childhood home and headed toward Rodeo Drive that he realized how much he was enjoying himself in this simple moment with her. No one was clamoring for a selfie or asking him questions. It was just the two of them with the wind blowing around them and the California sun beating down. Could he be happy like this forever or was this just another illusion he had created? One that would be a way to get over the guilt that had driven him from LA in the first place?

Lila was loving being in California, but she had to admit that what she loved most about it was being here with Zach. He was showing her his world and she relished it. When they'd driven past his childhood home, he hadn't stopped, just sort of gestured to it with a nod of his head and slowed down slightly.

She'd wanted to ask him about it, but he'd left the residential neighborhood of mansions behind and drove them to Rodeo Drive, pointing out some of the hills that had been damaged during the wildfires the year before. There was real pain in his voice as he talked about the devastation and the fear he'd felt as the fires spread in an unpredictable pattern.

She almost forgot about how he'd been so quiet at the house until they were seated for lunch at 208 Rodeo. The menu proclaimed it was Italian American fusion and she couldn't wait to see what that was. She had to admit there were things about California that she liked but there was no way this place would be better than Charlotte's cooking at Sheen.

They placed their order. Zach had asked for a seat overlooking both Rodeo and Wilshire and for the first time she understood the term *pretty people*. Because they were all around her. Walking, shopping and being seen.

"Is this everything you hoped it would be?" he asked.

"It's a bit fake, isn't it?"

He threw his head back and laughed. "Yeah, everyone is here for a reason."

"Not lunch, right? I mean it does seem like people have really...well, my mom would say *made an ef-*

fort. And she means when you take your time with your look and everything. Kind of like what I'm doing for my social media posts, but this is real life."

"It is," he said. "I think Rodeo really captures that aspirational lifestyle vibe. Of course, we'll make a few posts."

"Can't wait."

"OMG, is that Lila Jones? It is," a woman about twenty said as she came up to their table. "I love that photo you posted yesterday of that cute little coffee shop. I'm loving the vibe of your feed right now. So on point but not too in-your-face with retailers. Can I grab a selfie?"

"Sure," Lila said, standing up and putting her arm around the woman. "What's your name?"

"Kylie. I'm from Oklahoma and have been out here for about six months. Until I saw your feed, I didn't realize how much I missed home or how cool it could be."

Kylie snapped her photo and then noticed Zach. "Oh, you're really with ZB? That's awesome. I'm not really into the jet set but you are a total hottie.

"Take care of my girl," Kylie said with a wave as she walked away.

Lila sat back down and looked over at Zach. Feeling a little excitement and then embarrassed that she was excited at having someone recognize her. "I can't believe that just happened! Someone *recognized* me… I mean—here."

"I know. What did you think?" he asked.

"I liked it. I'm not going to lie. I can see why you are addicted to this lifestyle."

Zach leaned in close and her heart raced faster.

"Thinking about making this permanent?" he asked.

"What? I mean I couldn't. I'm just a novelty, right?" she asked, because she wasn't really sure of anything at this moment. Not this newfound celebrity. And especially not Zach. All she knew for sure was that her feelings for him were getting deeper with each day she spent with him.

"You are whatever you want this to be," he said, taking her hand in his. A shiver spread up her arm as it always did when he touched her. "It can be as real as you make it."

She nodded. "Like us?"

"I'm not sure what you mean."

"Are we as real as I make us," she said. "Or are we solid?"

"I showed you my childhood home. That's pretty deep," he reminded her.

"You did, but you didn't say anything," she said. "Was it a happy place for you? Do you miss it?"

"It was okay. I went to boarding school from the age of eight, so not too attached to that home. Prior to that, I was in a private school across town. Seems like most of my childhood until I went away to school was spent in the back of the Lincoln Town Car that Cissy drove."

She was learning more about him in this moment

than she had previously. How did this all fit into the man who lived his life in the spotlight? The LA bad boy who slept with other men's wives and made bets with shy, small-town girls and changed lives.

"Who is Cissy?" she asked.

"She was my nanny. Actually, she was an au pair from Limoges. She was pretty funny and I liked her. My dad did, too, so she left us after a year and my mom found a dour woman to watch me." Zach shrugged. "And to be honest, I can't even remember her name now."

Lila leaned forward across the table, taking Zach's hand in hers. The one woman that he'd been close to as a child had been taken from him. It kind of made her wonder if that was the reason he had a hard time making a real connection. Was this the missing piece she'd been searching for?

"I'm sorry." Her heart broke for his life. No wonder he needed the adulation of his followers. He'd been alone for so much of his formative years, there had to be something inside him that needed the attention. That gave her pause. Made her realize that he might never be able to step out of the spotlight.

"Ah, don't sweat it. I'm not a poor little rich boy," he said. "What about you? Happy childhood?"

"Yes. Really happy. Only child, and my parents spoiled me."

"Glad one of us had that. So, what do you want to do this afternoon?" he asked. "I got an invite for a party at an exclusive nightclub later tonight. It should be fun. Want to hit it?"

A party. Did she? Normally she wasn't—stop, she warned herself. She had to stop comparing herself to who she was and just go for it. Let her hair down and enjoy every moment of this.

"Yes. I mean I think so. I've never been to that kind of party."

"You'll love it," he promised. "We are going to set this town on fire, Brown Eyes. By the time tomorrow comes you'll be trending on the internet."

She sat back in her chair, smiling. She liked the sound of that. And she especially liked that she wasn't shy Lila Jones anymore. When she was with Zach, she felt like she was the exciting, vibrant woman in the social media feed that he'd created. And the more she lived this life, the more she was coming to love it and the man who'd brought her into it. Another part of her wondered if this could last.

After nearly four days being in California, Lila was really turning into a party animal. But this morning she had a meeting with burgeoning documentary filmmaker Abby Carmichael at a coffee shop near the Santa Monica Pier. She'd left Zach sleeping in his bed and driven the Mercedes C-Class convertible that Zach had told her to use while she was in California.

She spotted the documentary filmmaker immediately from her photo as she walked up to the café. She waved at Lila as she approached. Abby had long dark brown hair and a light brown complexion, and was wearing a thin flannel shirt paired with skinny jeans.

"Hi, Abby. I'm Lila. Thanks for meeting me in person." She had on her prescription sunglasses and was still slightly hungover from a party last night. But she was determined to use her newfound fame to help the Soiree. That was why she'd taken the bet, after all. Somehow that reason had faded the more time she spent with Zach. She had been finding it harder and harder to relate to her life in Royal as she'd been swept into Zach's world. To that end, she'd been ignoring calls from home because she didn't want her mom to tell her that it was time to stop this nonsense and come home.

"Nice to meet you," Abby said. "Um, I checked out the website for your event, but tell me more about it."

"Of course. The Soiree on the Bay is the brain-child of the Edmond family of Royal. So far, we have a lot of the members of the Texas Cattleman's Club involved. They are the elite, moneyed crowd."

"Sounds like there should be some good stories there. What about Zach Benning? Is he coming to the event with his posse?" she asked.

"Yes, he is," Lila said. "And we also have Kingston Blue and his entourage, who are always a lot of fun."

"You kind of have a following now, too, right?" Abby remarked.

"Yeah, but that's just kind of a subset of ZB's fans," Lila explained. She didn't want to build herself up too much. Especially since she still wasn't sure how long her followers would stick with her.

"ZB? I thought you two were a couple," Abby said.

Lila took a deep breath, looking at this woman with the clear gaze and the straightforward manner. She had her shit together in a way that Lila used to. This new lifestyle and California were confusing her. Making her want things that weren't really true to herself. On the drive to Santa Monica this morning she'd had plenty of time to think. And she'd started to realize that she wasn't getting closer to Zach, which had been what she'd hoped for when she'd agreed to take this trip home with him.

The parties were fun, of course. She had met people that she'd never thought she would even bump into at the airport. Talking to them had just made her more confused about Zach and herself and the life they had. The celebrities she'd talked to had either been all about themselves or genuinely real people gobsmacked by their fame.

Sure, they were sleeping together and the sex was hotter than ever and they partied every night and went to A-list events, but she'd learned more about him in five minutes that first day at lunch at 208 Rodeo than she had the last four days.

"We are together," Lila confirmed. "But it's complicated."

Abby laughed a little. "When isn't it when there is a man involved?"

Lila just shook her head. "I know. Normally I date guys that aren't...well, Zach."

"I'm sure you'll figure it out. You look like a woman who has her stuff together," Abby said.

Appearances can be deceiving, Lila thought. And it resonated with her.

"Thanks. I hope you'll come to Royal to film. I can get you access to the Edmond family and Billy Holmes—he's sort of an unofficial member of the family. Also we have a really cool chef, Charlotte Jarrett, who is overseeing the menus for the event. You'll have a lot of good people to talk to."

"Okay. I think this sounds like something interesting," Abby said. "Let me think about it, okay?"

They continued chatting over brunch and then Lila left her to drive back to Zach's place. Her phone was blowing up from the photo she'd posted of herself and Abby at the café and she shut it off. She was starting to feel fatigued from this. While she knew that somehow Zach thrived under the spotlight, it was taking a toll on her.

Or maybe it was simply the fact that when she was out with Zach they had to be photo-ready and always on for his followers and now hers. It was hard. Complicated.

Lila remembered her thought that appearances could be deceiving. She yearned for something simpler. Like playing spit in her living room with Zach.

Just the two of them in their most comfy clothes not staging the evening for followers.

She was pretty sure she'd been duping herself each morning when she looked in the mirror. Trying to convince herself that this new Lila was better than the old version of herself. But the truth was she was simply different. She was *tired*. Lila hadn't wanted to admit it to herself, but she was tired of faking it for others. And she just realized she had been faking it as much as she'd been genuinely enjoying it. She wanted Zach to think she could fit into his life. But had she lost herself for him?

No.

She enjoyed this feeling of being free and living in the moment.

But it couldn't last forever. Nor did she want it to. She wanted to go home to Royal…with Zach…and have her new image in her hometown. But this glitzy, hard-partying world that he was a part of? It wasn't for her. And that was the problem. She wasn't sure that Zach could want the quiet life that she craved.

The May California sun was bright and should be cheering her up, but as she turned onto Zach's street in Beverly Hills, she knew it wasn't. That this was never going to feel right or feel like home.

Maybe if she and Zach were *more*. If he truly cared about her and she felt like together they had something real, then she could enjoy this. But whenever she got too real, Zach backed away.

Was that it?

She decided it was. When she got back to his place she was going to talk to him, to figure out what was happening between them, because she wasn't willing to keep going like this. She missed her quiet neighborhood and the Texas heat. She missed just eating a meal when it was still hot and not making sure she posted it for the world to see. But she also knew she would miss Zach if he didn't come back with her.

Somehow when she'd been changing herself, something real had emerged and it wasn't just her love for high fashion. She had started to really care for Zach Benning. The vulnerable man behind the bad-boy image that he was always rolling out for his posts.

She had to find out if that man was real and if he cared about her, too. And that was what she was determined to do today.

Thirteen

Zach woke alone to find a note from Lila telling him she'd gone to take a meeting with a documentary filmmaker. He scrubbed his hand over his face, felt the stubble that had grown in overnight and tried to force himself to look at his phone. He had been nonstop partying, giving Lila the lifestyle that she'd sounded so excited about that first day. But to be honest, he was tired and somehow having her by his side was making it harder to keep up the illusion that his life was perfect.

He especially felt the hollowness in it with her here with him in California. He wondered if it was because she was too real. Too Texas for this life. He had no doubt that she would have already sent a thank-you gift to the host of last night's party. It was the talk of his set that she did it. Everyone felt that it was an anachronism but at the same time appreciated the thoughtful gifts she sent along.

And they were well-thought-out gifts. He had overheard her talking to Lil Dominator last night about his kids, and he suspected that Lila would include a gift for them when she sent his thank-you gift. She genuinely cared about people. He recalled her telling him that all those years of blending into the background had made her a good listener. And that was 100 percent true. People liked to talk to her and now that his spotlight was on her as well, she hadn't stopped listening.

But he had. He'd never been good at it. Frankly if something didn't involve him, he'd never seen the point in it. But this was Lila and she might be more important to him than anyone had been since his French au pair. Which was sad but also very true.

He showered and shaved and wondered if she'd go for a quiet day at home just lounging by the pool. He wanted to talk to her. To be the one that she was listening to. It had been all about her since they arrived, and he needed some of her attention just for him.

Zach blew out a breath. He had a lot of DMs to go through but he wasn't ready to deal with them until he had coffee and maybe something to eat.

"Morning, Mrs. Smith," he said as he breezed into the kitchen. "What do we have to eat?"

"Breakfast burrito?" she asked.

"Perfect, and a large coffee. I'll take it by the pool, maybe with some of that fresh fruit salad you made yesterday, too?"

"Certainly. I'll get it right out to you," she said.

He walked through the house, realizing how quiet it was without Lila by his side. She was always sharing what was on her mind and talking to him about the upcoming Soiree on the Bay and, well, everything. Yesterday she'd told him about an article she'd read about Los Angeles when it had been just orange groves everywhere.

He missed it…missed her.

He wasn't about to let this continue. Somehow, he had to get her to focus on him and then this empty void would go away. She was stirring feelings that it was getting harder and harder to deny he had for her. Feelings that he didn't want to name because frankly he wasn't a lovable man. He knew that. Had known it from the time he was very young. He had always been too blunt, too self-focused, too *Zach*.

He sat down and noticed that Lila had posted a new photo. She looked good, a bit fatigued but still good. Some of the sparkle that he'd noticed in her early photos wasn't there. But her likes were larger than ever so her followers weren't catching on.

He'd seen another protégé of his self-destruct and completely go off-grid. Lila was made of stronger stuff and that would never happen with her, but at the same time he was concerned.

He didn't know how to move them forward. And

a part of him was afraid to see if he had anything to offer her without the social media boost. Would she still like him when she tired of this? And he *hated* that he was worrying about it.

He was Zach fucking Benning, not some wimpy, insecure dude who couldn't keep a woman. That was the damned feelings. He knew it. He needed to stop obsessing over how he felt about her and just do him.

Sex.

Parties.

A fabulous life.

That was it. That was what he had to give her. She could come along for the ride or not. He wasn't going to let himself get drawn further into this downward spiral.

Mrs. Smith dropped off his breakfast and Zach refused to look at Lila's social media account anymore. He was going to go back to being himself.

He'd allowed himself to be drawn into this coupledom thing without thinking it through. He was smarter than that. He DMed a few of his most loyal followers and set up a party that night for just them. Something exclusive on his yacht that he kept moored in Marina del Rey. He'd bring Lila along, but starting tonight, he had to put some distance between them.

She was becoming too important to him. And he knew that once she got over the novelty of this life, she was going to start to look harder at him, and Zach was afraid she'd see who he really was.

A hedonistic man who lived for his own pleasure.

Not a man she wanted to spend the next week with, much less the rest of her life.

Hell, did he want the rest of her life?

He shook his head. That wasn't the kind of thing someone as self-absorbed as he would want.

But he did, he thought.

When she walked through the patio door a few hours later, he realized that no matter what lies he wanted to tell himself, the truth was that he wanted her. Not just in his bed but also in his heart. He wanted that with his entire soul.

Lila sat down across from Zach and put her Birkin on the table next to her. She was never going to admit it, but she loved the bag that he had given her way more than her old canvas messenger bag. Mostly because she remembered the look on his face as she'd opened it and how he'd teased her about her "beast" of a bag. In fact, there was a lot that he'd given her that she loved.

"How'd the meeting go?" Zach asked.

"Great. She's going to come to Royal soon I think," Lila said. "I told her all about the main players and she thought there would be a lot to work with. She asked about you…so I imagine she'll want to interview you."

"You know I love the camera."

"I do," she said with a smirk. The paparazzi were at every party and event they attended. At first, she was just an unnamed partner for him but then they had found out her name, too.

"Your post is doing good. I almost feel like I don't have anything left to teach you."

"Is it?" she asked. "I turned off my phone. It's always blowing up and honestly, I needed a break. Don't you?"

"Not really," he said.

She pulled her phone out and turned it on, waiting for it to boot up. There was a note in his voice that made her wonder if he was being honest about that. But before she could ask him about it, her phone was back on and she saw she had seven missed calls from her dad and twenty-one from her mom. There was a text message from both of them that read simply: URGENT. Call home.

"Oh, my God. I think something happened," she said. "I have to call my parents."

"Okay. Do you want me to go inside to give you some privacy?"

"I really don't want to get bad news alone. Would you mind staying?"

"Not at all," he said, reaching over to take her free hand as she pushed the button to dial her mom's phone.

"Lila Jones. Where have you been? I've been trying to reach you all day," her mom said as she answered the phone.

"I just turned the phone off. Mom, what's wrong?" she asked. And, truthfully, she'd been ignoring her mom's texts and calls because she hadn't wanted to face reality. Hadn't wanted to think about the fact that she missed home. That she knew deep inside that there was probably no way to move forward with Zach. He didn't miss Texas or what they'd had there.

"Winifred Williams passed away on Friday. I tried to call you then. Her funeral was today," her mom said. "You were one of her favorite people, Lila. I thought you'd want to be there. And it looks like all you've been doing is hanging out and drinking with that Zach guy."

"Mom, I'm so sorry," she said, tears burning in her eyes as she thought of Winifred being gone. That sweet older lady had been like a great-auntie to Lila. She'd been the one to nurture her love of books. "I can't believe I missed her funeral. I didn't mean to not call you back, but with the time difference…"

She stopped talking because it sounded like an excuse, like a lie even to her own ears. "I didn't call you back because I didn't want to talk to anyone from home. I was afraid you'd point out that I don't fit in out here."

"Well, you did miss the funeral. If you'd looked at your phone it wouldn't have happened," her mom said. "Why would I say you didn't fit in? You changed for yourself, right? Not for a man."

Her mother was mad at her and Lila couldn't blame her. But she was also saying all the things that Lila needed to hear. "I did change for me, but it's overwhelming, Mom. I can't believe Winifred is gone—"

She had to stop talking because she had started crying and her throat had sort of closed up and no matter how she tried to talk all that came out was a sort of sob. Zach took the phone from her, rubbing her back as he did so.

"Mrs. Jones, this is Zach Benning…Fair enough… I'm sorry, ma'am. I will get her home today. It's my fault that she missed the calls from you. You know how much of herself Lila puts into her job. She was trying to make as many connections for the Soiree as she could."

He listened and nodded as he continued to rub her back. "I know she does work too hard."

But she didn't. No matter what Zach said, she knew she should have seen those messages and responded to them. She held her hand out for her phone.

"Lila wants to talk to you again," Zach told her mom. "I'll see you soon. Again, I'm sorry for my part in this."

He handed her back her phone and then reached for his own.

"Mom, I'm sorry."

"Me, too, sweetie. I should have realized you were working hard and trying to do everything to help the Soiree. I know that's why you went out there." Her mom sighed. "But we were worried about you. Some of the pictures we've seen online looked like you were partying hard."

"A little bit, but that's where the A-listers hang out," she said, but inside it felt like a lie. She'd been having fun as much as she'd been talking up the Soiree. She couldn't hide from that. And a dear lady that she'd loved had passed and been buried and Lila hadn't been home for it. She'd been so caught up in living the Hollywood life and being what Zach needed her to be that she'd missed something that was important to her.

"I'm glad you are coming home. Zach said he'd arrange a flight for you today. Coffee tomorrow to catch up and then we can go to the cemetery and put some flowers on Winifred's grave?"

"Yes. That sound fine to me. I'll message you when I'm home."

"Safe travels, honey. Sorry I was rude about Zach," she said. "Love you."

"Love you, too, Mom," she murmured as she hung up the phone.

Zach put his phone down as she finished the call with her mom. He was watching her with the most serious look she'd ever seen on his face. She wondered if she'd gotten too real for him, crying like she had. It hadn't escaped her notice that he didn't do emotion, not really. Sexy feelings yes, but anything too real, too deep, he shied away from.

"I've got the pilot getting the jet ready. We can leave as soon as we get to the airport. I'm sorry you missed the funeral."

"Thanks," she said. What she was doing out here?

It was as if she was just waking up from the glitter-covered fantasy she'd fallen into. The lifestyle and the environment that had seemed so fun when she'd gotten here now felt draining and fake.

"What's the matter?" he asked.

"I'm just wondering what I'm doing here."

"Building word of mouth for your Soiree. Spending time with me. Having fun."

"This isn't real. None of this is. I don't know what I was thinking," she said, standing up.

Zach turned to her with a frown. "I'm real, Brown Eyes. And so are you. Don't beat yourself up over one missed hometown event."

"It's not a missed event. It was the funeral of a woman who was like a granny to me. She was important and real."

Zach was a little bit offended at the way she was dismissing him, mainly because he felt her slipping away. This had been his chance to see if he could hold on to something solid, something real, and not a photographed image of the perfect life he'd concocted for his followers. "This *is* real. I don't know how you can't see it."

"To you," she said. "This isn't me. Somehow I forgot that."

"Isn't it?" he asked. "I have my private jet lined up to take you back to Texas. Will that be real enough for you?"

"Don't be a jerk. I wasn't insulting you," she said.

But she had.

"Sure, whatever," he retorted. "I'm going to go with you, so I need to pack a bag and get things lined up for myself in Royal."

"Zach, I'm sorry if I sounded ungrateful," she said. "It's just—don't you get tired of being *on* all the time?"

"I don't. I live for it. This is what makes me feel alive," he admitted, turning and walking back to her. "And if you are being completely honest with yourself, you'll admit that you like it, too."

"I do like it. But that doesn't make it something solid," she said.

"But it is," he reminded her. "Was Lil Dominator not real? His kids and that conversation with him?"

"That's not fair. Of course the people are real," she said. "I wasn't saying that."

"No, you weren't. You were trying to point out that your lifestyle is somehow more grounded because you work at the chamber of commerce and my taking photos of my life and helping people escape their everyday routine with my posts isn't."

He knew he was hitting this too hard, but it was like all the stuff he'd been thinking about her was now coming out. Lila didn't like him or his lifestyle. She found it shallow and probably thought the same about him. He was seeing her and feeling like his life could change for the better with her in it, and she was writing him off.

"No, I wasn't," she said. "That's not fair. Your life

is hard. Even you have to see that it's not perfect. How do you handle having to get up every day and make the perfect post?"

"It's a job," he pointed out.

"Touché."

"I'm not trying to one-up you. I like you, Lila. I like this thing we've got going," he said. "I don't want it to end."

She nodded at that. "I don't see how it could continue. I can't live out here. I don't think I even want to."

"Okay. That's fair. But are there options?"

She shook her head. "I don't know. I think we are very different people. You were right when you said I enjoyed talking to Lil Dominator and getting to know his family. But that's not why you go to those events. Honestly, I'm a little tired of it."

He wanted to tell her he could change, but he knew he wouldn't. This was his reality. Yes, his social media girlfriend was breaking up with him. He'd find another.

But a part of him didn't want to. He wasn't ready to let go of Lila Jones.

"What is so bad about this?" he asked. "You like the clothes and the bags and the—"

He felt defensive and he knew he was using the luxury merchandise as a front. He wanted her to like *him*. Didn't she like him? Or was she following the same pattern as everyone else in his life? Was he not enough? Hell.

"Stop. It was fun, but it's not me. I'm pretending

to be a version of myself that I don't like. I'm not this woman. As much as I like the stuff, it's just stuff. And I like my parents and Royal and you more. I like *you*, Zach. The real man, not ZB, and I want to figure out a way to have a life with you but not if you can't be real with me. I'm not sure that to you I'm anything other than this @LilaJones persona you created."

Her words stung. He liked the woman she was now. But he hadn't not liked her before. He might have started out wanting her to change so that he could feel better about sleeping with her and going back to his life afterward. But that had changed. *He'd* changed. He hadn't wanted to, and honestly, he still wasn't sure about it. Especially not now when she was saying she didn't like anything about this world.

"You are more than that. I think you are trying to deflect the guilt you feel about not returning those calls. But the truth is more complex than you want it to be. As much as you think I'm just about the posts and the paparazzi, you know that you liked this life. You liked being out here and standing in the spotlight with me."

God, please let that be true. He'd thought that they were starting to be a real couple. That's why he'd planned a party—he'd gotten scared and wanted to put distance between them—but now that she was talking about leaving, he realized he didn't want her to go.

"I liked being with you in Royal, too," she said quietly.

He hadn't liked it. Being there, being with Lila, stirred too much. Too many old desires and feelings that he'd learned to live without.

"That's not my life. Take my jet and go back to your home but never pretend that I only liked you because I made you into someone who would fit my profile. I liked you before you agreed to the make-over. You might want to ask yourself why you did that."

She shook her head but didn't say anything else and he turned and strode into the house. He asked Mrs. Smith to have his driver take Lila to the corporate airport where his jet was kept and then went into his private study and closed the door behind him.

He needed to shake this off. This was no different than Tawny getting out of his Ferrari in Royal and walking away from him. But he'd never lied to himself before and he didn't want to start now. He was going out and he was going to find another woman and in a few hours, he wouldn't even remember Lila Jones.

But that lie was hard to swallow. He knew the instant she left his house because he felt as if the air had been sucked out of it. No matter how he was going to act on social media, losing Lila had hurt. And he would've tried to fight for her but she'd been right. He was as hollow as his lifestyle.

Letting her go back to the life she loved was the honorable thing to do. He sneered at himself. The man who'd always put himself first had finally let someone else have the spotlight by themselves. He would miss her. Not just today but whenever he remembered this time in his life when he'd had something good and solid but had been too cowardly to hold on to her. Because he'd been afraid if he let her in, she'd see that the real man was a hollow version of the ZB he sold online.

He poured himself a Jack Daniel's neat and downed it in one swallow. Yeah, he was going to get drunk and party like nothing had changed tonight. He canceled the meetup with his followers and texted his hard-partying friends instead. He needed a few nights of oblivion and then he'd figure out his next move.

Fourteen

Lila was still tired when her mom rang her doorbell at 8:00 a.m. the next morning. She had cried most of the way home on the plane trying to find peace with the decision she'd made to leave Zach. She knew it was the right thing to do. They couldn't continue the way they had been. But it still hurt.

She opened the door to her mom, who had a travel coffee cup in her hand and gave it to Lila before hugging her. She saw over her mom's shoulder that her dad was sitting in the car. Even though she'd thought she'd been doing a good job of getting herself together she started crying again.

"Sweetheart, what's the matter?" her mom said.

Lila heard her dad turn off the car as she sat down

on the rocking chair on her front porch. "I'm sorry I wasn't here for Winifred and that I let you down."

"You didn't let us down. I was a little harsh," her mom admitted.

"She was. But we were worried about you," her dad said as he joined them. He leaned down and hugged her and she stood up to embrace him back because her dad gave the best hugs.

Lila was still crying and had to admit to herself that it was about more than disappointing her parents and missing Winifred's funeral. She wanted to go back to a world where she knew how to handle everything. Bottom line? She hadn't realized how different her life would be when she let Zach into it, and how much he would change not just her public persona but also her.

"I'm sorry about that."

"How about we go put those flowers on Winifred's grave and then go home and I'll make my famous blueberry pancakes," her dad suggested.

"Okay. Let me lock up."

Two hours later she was sitting in her parents' kitchen somehow telling her mom and dad all about Zach. They'd been to Winifred's grave and eaten her dad's pancakes and now she was still a little weepy but getting herself together.

"So, what does he do again?" her dad asked. "I don't see how posting stuff is a way to make a living."

"I didn't, either, but he has a huge number of followers and most of them want to have this glitzy life-style, so they are willing to buy a few products or go places that he talks about," Lila said. "He's done a lot for the Soiree, really helped to drive up not only word of mouth but ticket sales."

"Okay, well then, what's the problem?" her dad asked. "I can tell you really like this boy and he's got a job."

"Leo, there are important things other than a job and liking him," her mom said.

"Well, not every man can have my special talents of being charming, sexy and supersmart."

Her mom shook her head and playfully smacked him. Lila smiled, too. Her dad had gotten straight to the heart of the matter. What *was* the issue?

"He lives in LA, for one. The other is that he really likes that entire lifestyle he's selling, and I don't mind taking a few pictures now and then but I want something a little quieter. I mean, I really like him, but we are just too different."

She had hoped they weren't. That after she laid it all on the line that he'd want to be real with her. Find a life away from his Benningnites. But she'd gotten on that plane by herself and come back to Texas.

Which pretty much said it all, right?

"That's too bad, sweetie," her mom said. "I wish it were different."

"Me, too," she admitted. "But it's not. And even though I'm sitting here like I have nothing to do all day, I do need to head into work. Would you mind driving me home?"

"Not at all," her dad said. "Want to come for dinner tonight?"

"Sorry, I can't." She was meeting the advisory committee later on to bring them up to speed on her meeting with Abby, and also needed to fill them in on the new ticket sales thanks to Zach's online posts about Soiree on the Bay. "Working on the event."

"Well, then over the weekend. I'll text you," her mom told her.

"Thanks," she said, hugging her mom and dad. As she did she realized that Zach had never had this. That he didn't trust in anything other than followers because that was the only time he'd had some kind of affection other than in the sack. She wondered if there was a way to show him how special and extraordinary love could be coming from one person instead of from the masses.

That thought was in the back of her mind as she went back into the office. Everyone commented on the parties she'd attended and the photos she'd posted. They wanted to know all the details of her glam time in LA.

She shared it with them but kept the details of her time with Zach to herself. That was private, and she realized that she'd seen him do that with the two of them, as well. Maybe she'd overlooked something... or was she just grasping at straws, trying her best to get back together with him because she'd never had a broken heart before?

"Is Zach here with you?" one of her coworkers asked.

"No, he had to stay in LA for some events he had lined up. But I'm sure we will see him at the Soiree."

"I can't believe we are only like a month away. This event is really coming together. You did a great job," her coworker raved.

"Thanks," she said, but she knew she wouldn't have been half as effective without the social media and personal makeover that Zach had given her. He'd introduced her to people she'd never have met without him. She could say that he'd made her into someone he wanted to like but she knew those words had come from her own fears. She'd wanted to be someone who fit into his world, but then she'd been afraid to stay there.

And her biggest regret? That she'd never had the courage to tell him she loved him because she was afraid that she really didn't fit in his life. Could never be the kind of woman he would love.

Zach lay on the deck of his yacht moored at the yacht club in Marina del Ray. He had tried to drink Lila off his mind but that hadn't worked. He couldn't stop thinking about what she'd said. She wanted him to be real for her. In fact, he'd done all of his usual moving-on tricks, picked up a hot chick and tried to hook up but he'd called her Lila as he was kissing her and she'd pulled back. He'd left her with some friends and come here.

Where he could be alone. His team were at the house and had all been trying to reach out to him but he wasn't in the mood to talk. What was he going to say? It seemed as if he'd screwed up the one thing that might have been real in this life of his.

He wanted to figure out a way forward but honestly, he had been doing this for so long that he had no clue how to move on.

"Dude, please tell me you are at least wearing massive amounts of sunscreen," Shantal said as her shadow fell over him. He looked up to see his makeup artist flanked by Dawn and Vito.

"Of course, I'm not a total idiot," he muttered.

"Just a partial one, right? I mean, I assume this is because we're here and Lila is in Texas," Vito said, sitting down on the lounger next to Zach. Vito had on a baseball cap, linen pants and a long-sleeved linen shirt.

"Maybe," he admitted. "So why are you guys here?"

"You need us. Or maybe, more precisely, you need Lila," Dawn said, pushing his legs to the side and sitting down on the end of his lounger as Shantal did the same to Vito.

"She doesn't like this lifestyle."

"Do *you*?" Shantal asked. "We know you like the adoring followers and the parties, but you were different when she was out here. It seemed sort of…"

"Like you were finally growing up and realizing there was more to life than partying," Dawn said. "If I'm out of line, fine."

She wasn't out of line and he suspected she knew it. "You're right. But I have no idea how to show her that."

"You'll think of something, boss," Vito assured him. "You're smart when you're not being dumb."

Zach laughed for the first time in days. His team weren't just employees, he realized, but also friends who understood him. "I've been thinking about how to win her back and the future. What do you guys think of a sort of brand company who does what we did for Lila but for businesses? I'd need my number one team with me."

"OMG! I love it," Shantal exclaimed. "But how would it work?"

"We'd give our clients social media makeovers, help connect them to influencers that they want to work with or help mold someone from their company into the influencer they want them to be."

"Yes, that will work," Dawn said.

"Now what are you going to do about Lila?" Vito prodded. "She's going to be a hell of a lot harder to win back."

"I have a few ideas, guys. But I'm going to have to do this on my own," he said.

"All alone?" Shantal pouted. "I was hoping we could all head back to Texas."

"Oh, no worries, we're all going to Royal. I'm

going to base the new business there. And I really could use some help finding a permanent house."

"Mrs. Smith and I already found a few that we think you'll like," Dawn informed him. He shook his head as he looked over at her. "What? It's not like I had much else to do since you've gone completely silent on social media. Which I have to say is making the gossip sites and your fans go wild. They are sure you are announcing something big."

He almost laughed. Even when he tried to disappear it just continued to feed the need for him in the media spotlight. He was going to have to try very hard to convince Lila that he'd changed. This might look like a gimmick to her. But he wanted her to know he was real.

Which meant he was going to have to just strip back all the layers he'd been using for years to build his following and his influence. He was going to have to be humble and show her that there was one thing that mattered to him in this world, and it was her.

Zach was pretty sure that he loved her. Hell, he *knew* he did. He'd been hedging around her and pretending that he didn't know what the emotion was but only because he'd never said those words to anyone since he'd been an adult. And he knew he was going to have to tell her how he felt.

"If I can't win Lila back…I still want to stay based in Royal. There's a lot of good stuff happening there, and we'll be centrally located for the entire US."

"That's fine with me, boss," Vito said. "I've been looking for a change."

"Me, too," Shantal concurred. "And my mom lives in Dallas, so she'll be over the moon that I'm closer to her. And Dawn has her own reasons..."

"What?"

"I met a guy at the diner. We've been texting. It might be something, I don't know. I mean, moving there is a good thing but I'm not moving *for* him."

As Zach chatted with his friends, it struck him that his life wasn't as hollow as he'd thought it was. His heart started racing. All along he had thought he'd been protecting himself and keeping everyone at arm's length, but saw now that wasn't true. He'd created some strong bonds over the years, and he knew that what he'd felt and found with Lila was solid, too. He just had to get her attention the *right* way this time.

And he had an idea how to accomplish that. In fact, the more he thought about it, the more he loved it.

He told the team and they all were surprised but thought it would work, too. Now he just had to get back to Royal and pray that it wasn't too late to convince Lila he loved her.

Lila got dressed in one of the outfits that she'd gotten with Zach, realizing how much she had enjoyed their time together, and drove her new red VW convertible to meet the advisory committee. She'd decided to trade in Milo for a new car because she'd always wanted a convertible and she was tired of denying herself. She'd kept the group apprised of everything that had gone on in California in their group chat, but they were getting together for some drinks and to finalize some details tonight.

She took a photo of herself, tagged the brands she was wearing and used #SoireeontheBay before leaving. Gina and Valencia were there when she arrived, and she ordered a skinny margarita from the bar before joining them.

"California looks like it was good to you," Valencia said after she'd sat down.

"I tried to make the most of my time there. Everyone was really interested in the event and thought we were doing something groundbreaking," she replied. "And the best part? Lil Dominator is going to come, and he offered to perform if we have room on one of the stages." She'd really enjoyed meeting him and his wife Tisha. They had texted her photos of the kids playing on the ride-on mustangs she'd sent them.

"That's great. Zach's notoriety has really given the Soiree a boost. I hope he will continue to keep it going," Gina said.

She nodded. "I'm sure he will."

Really, what else could she say?

"Is he coming tonight?"

"Uh, not tonight. He had to stay in LA."

"Really?" Charlotte murmured as she joined

them. "His account has gone dark. The social world is all abuzz about what's coming next from him."

"It is? He's probably got a new account or brand partnership he's going to announce. He never does anything without a plan," she said.

"Who doesn't?" Jack asked.

"Zach," she said. "How have you been? How's Lexi?"

"I'm good and so is she," Jack answered, turning to Charlotte. "How's Ross?"

"Good. He's doing good," Charlotte said.

"I can't believe that he is still estranged from Dad," Gina lamented.

Lila couldn't, either. But then men didn't always make sense to her. "You'd think standing up and being a father to little Ben would have been something that Rusty would support."

"You'd think," Charlotte said. "But there is a lot of ego to Rusty and he likes to think he runs the world."

"Ha. So true. To be honest I wish I ran the world," Jack quipped. "But Lexi keeps me grounded."

Billy showed up and they all chatted about the event and life stuff while they waited for Rusty. Lila only half paid attention to the conversation, pulling out her phone to check Zach's account. Not only had it gone dark, it had been suspended.

That worried her. What was going on with him? She told herself she was going to give it some time to try to figure out what to do next but what if he needed her? Heck, forget waiting. Zach loved all of his followers and to shut down his account, something had to have happened. She texted him.

Hey, hope you are okay.

I'm good.

Well, there it was. That wasn't exactly a chatty invitation for more texts but she couldn't let it go.

I'd love to talk sometime.

Me, too. Can't now.

Okay. Text when you can.

He gave her message a thumbs-up and that was it.

Lila tried not to feel sad that this was what they were reduced to. She still cared so much for him. And while she was trying to be strong and move on, this was a sign, right? It had to be. She sent him a text and he sent back a thumbs-up. *Let him go, girl.*

The rest of the committee were laughing and talking about stuff at the Texas Cattleman's Club, trying to stretch out the conversation while they waited for Rusty.

Then Charlotte did a double take toward the door and they all turned to see what had caught her attention. Lila was shocked to see Ross walking toward them with his father by his side.

Billy got up first. "Ross, great to see you. This is a surprise."

Charlotte went to her man and gave him a sort of quizzical look, but he just kissed her and took her hand in his.

"Sorry we are late," Rusty said.

"I'm just glad to see you both here," Lila told them.

"Me, too," Gina agreed. "Lila has some news—"

"Before we get to that," Rusty interrupted. "Ross has something you all need to know."

Lila didn't like the sound of that. Seems like there was something going on that none of them had an inkling about. It must be something big for Rusty to have brought his estranged son to the meeting, because despite them showing up together it didn't seem as if they were super close now. But Lila wasn't privy to the inner workings of the Edmond family.

Ross took a deep breath, putting his hands on his hips. "There is money missing from the festival's bank account."

"*What?* Are you sure?" Jack asked. "I haven't turned in my last invoice. Do you think there is something you missed?"

"I'm sure and I haven't missed anything. Someone has been stealing from the account."

What did that mean for the Soiree? "Will it affect the festival?"

"Yes, I think it will. We need to find out who has taken the money and put an end to it," Rusty said.

Lila listened to the others who discussed what the

next steps were. She had no part in the money so she wasn't sure she could add anything. When the meeting finally broke up, she was a little worried about why someone would steal from the festival.

Was it simply that they thought no one would notice? And who would be ballsy enough to take from a charity event? That was simply creepy.

She went home unable to think of much besides this new development and Zach. He hadn't texted her again. What did *that* mean? She hoped it wasn't that he was over her and had moved on. Not now, when she was ready to do whatever it took to win him back.

Fifteen

Lila got an account recommendation when she checked her phone the next morning for @LJLVR21. It sounded like one of those spambot accounts, but she clicked on it anyway while she was making her breakfast and getting ready for work.

The feed looked very similar to how hers used to pre-Zach. There weren't many photos and the most recent was one of a stoneware mug that had the state of Texas on the side of it and a heart where Royal was with a teabag in it. The caption read: "Left my heart in Texas. Going back to find it."

How cute. There were two other photos on the account. One of a breakfast plate with just crumbs from some kind of pastry and the other of a slightly askew photo of the Hollywood sign. She clicked follow and then immediately felt a pang for Zach and his California life.

Enough of this missing Zach. She had somehow made herself believe that without her makeover she wouldn't have been enough for him. And maybe she hadn't been. But she *loved* Zach. She wanted him in her life. Thinking about how different they were actually made them so good as a couple. The fact that she wasn't like all the other people in his life, and that he wasn't like the ones in hers, made them unique and special. And ultimately, it came down to one undeniable truth: she was crazy about him and was tired of acting like they couldn't be together.

Lila texted him but it was undeliverable.

Uh, what?

Had he *blocked* her?

Well, that was going to make getting back together with him hard. She'd insulted his lifestyle, to be fair. Maybe he had gone dark because he was moving on. Moving away from the life he'd had because of her?

Lila wasn't sure but knew it would have to wait until she got to work. She was running late and there had been an email from Rusty to the festival advisory committee with some questions about expenses and who had access to the account. It seemed that he was determined to get to the bottom of who had taken the money.

She wanted to respond to him as soon as she was

at her desk. And sure hoped he didn't think it was her. After all, she'd been wearing a lot of expensive clothing that she couldn't afford on her salary and bought herself a brand-new car. She might have to explain how brands worked with influencers to him the way she had with her dad.

She was mentally composing her email to him when she pulled up in front of the chamber of commerce building. Glancing at the coffee shop, she saw the regulars at their tables and then a guy in the corner with hair that was the same shade of brown as Zach's. But Zach would never be out in public in the jeans and slouchy T-shirt that guy had on. Also he had on some sort of bucket hat with a pair of large blue-lensed sunglasses.

Dude, she thought. He needed some tips on how to style it up.

She parked her car and tried not to stare at the guy as she walked inside the coffee shop to get her morning cuppa. But the closer she got, the harder it was not to gawk. Unless she missed her guess, that guy was Zach.

She stopped thinking about the email she needed to send, her heart beating faster as she walked over to his table.

"Zach?"

"Hiya, Lila," he said with a tentative smile. "I was hoping to catch you before work."

She pulled out a chair and sat down. He took off the sunglasses and as soon as their eyes met she felt that electric thrill go through her as it always did when she was with him. God, she'd missed this man. But what the heck was he wearing?

"Hey, what are you doing here dressed like this? Are you okay?" she asked with a laugh. He looked so silly and so sweet and her pulse sped up as she tried to figure out what this meant. Zach never did anything without a plan.

He tried to look…well, if she were being honest, he tried to *be* less himself. He kept sitting up straight and then seemed to remember something and then slouched and leaned over himself. As if he were trying to keep himself small so no one would notice him. Which was so not Zach that she almost laughed.

"I'm here for you. I heard what you said. That we are too different, but I've changed. Look at me. I'm like you were. Just a regular Zach blending in."

She shook her head. "You could never blend in. You're not meant to. When I said real, I mean the real Zach and the real Lila. I want you to be that larger-than-life man who loves the spotlight and selfies but also…" She trailed off. For a minute she had to stop and gather all her courage. It took a lot to tell Zach that she loved him. But she was going to do it. *Also a man who loves me*, she thought.

Before she could say the words, he started talking.

"I'm trying to show you something and because I'm who I am it's harder than I thought."

"What are you trying to show me?" she asked.

"If my lifestyle isn't right for you then I have come

to realize that it's not right for me. I do like attention and the spotlight and yes, everything is usually about me, but I don't like me without you."

She held her breath, almost afraid for him to continue. "I like you."

"I know you do, Brown Eyes. I love you."

He breathed in deeply after he said it, the next words coming out in a rush.

"I tried to convince myself that it was only the novelty of you, but the truth is you have made me see the spots in my life where I was doing things to try to feel alive."

"Try to?" she asked. "What do you mean?"

"I mean that if I hadn't come to Royal, I would have been content to keep partying and sleeping with hotties and just going about that life. Not really looking around me and noticing things like pretty brunettes with sassy attitudes or the sunset or the flowers around me. You made me wake up and see that I was filling my days with so much stuff and standing in the spotlight because I wanted the world to see me.

"And *you're* real, Lila. You want me to be real, too. I've been afraid of that for so long. But I want to be real with you."

Being back in Royal was different than it had been before. He remembered how arrogant and sure of himself he'd been when he'd arrived. A bad boy running from a scandal of his own making. He'd come a long way since then and he knew it was because of Lila's influence. Regardless of what she said back to him, his life had been changed for good by her.

Zach had laid it on the line and kept talking, but now he had run out of words. He'd told her he loved her, and she hadn't said it back. His heart was racing like it never had before. It was all he could do to keep from pulling her into his arms and kissing her. *Thoroughly.* Then, if she was willing, he'd scoop her up and whisk her away to someplace private where he could make love to her. And he knew it would be making love, not just sex.

Because it was Lila Jones. The woman he'd made over but who had truly transformed him.

"Zach, I like your true self. You are such a generous, caring man. And I've changed, too. Realized that I was sort of just existing and not living. You showed me how to make the most of every moment. I love you, too," she said at last. "In more ways than you'll *ever* know. But I can't go back to California. That life is not for me."

Yes! She loved him. He didn't listen to the rest; he'd heard the only thing he needed to hear. They would sort this out but right now he needed to hold her. To make sure that she didn't change her mind. He stood up and pulled her to her feet and into his arms, kissing her long and deep, not caring if the morning commuters saw them.

She clung to him, holding on to his shoulders, and when he lifted his head, he saw in her eyes the sincerity of the love she'd professed. His heart felt full for the first time in his life.

"I didn't know how much I needed you until you were gone," he whispered as he pressed his forehead to hers. "I love you."

He hadn't meant to say the words again, but they were right there. The emotion so real that it was making him want to do and say things that he'd never considered before.

"I love you, too. Oh, Zach. I thought you'd moved on when you switched off your account," she said.

"I switched it off and created a new profile because my life is with you and not for my followers."

"Really?"

"Yes, really," he said.

"How will you make a living?" she asked, stepping back.

He laughed as joy filled him. She was so practical, his little Lila Jones. "I don't have to work to support myself, but I'm going to be starting a Texas-based brand makeover company to help businesses and folks who want to grow their social media presence. The team insisted on coming with me. We are going to be right here in Royal."

"Are you sure? I don't want you to do this and then regret it," she said.

"I am sure. From the moment you ran into me and I held you in my arms right across the street in front of the chamber of commerce, I knew you were different and I wasn't sure what that meant at first.

But over the last month you have opened my eyes to so much that I had missed before. I can't wait to see what the future holds for us." He tipped her chin up and stared into her eyes. "Will you marry me, Lila? Help me start a new life filled with love and experiences that aren't for the masses but just for *us*?"

"Yes!" she said, throwing herself back into his arms.

The people around them applauded and he kissed her again.

She called in sick to work and they spent the day in her little house making love and making plans for their future together, living in their authentic selves in the real world.

* * * * *

Don't miss the next book in the Texas Cattleman's Club: Heir Apparent series:
Texas Tough
by USA TODAY *bestselling author*
Janice Maynard

WE HOPE YOU ENJOYED
THIS BOOK FROM

HARLEQUIN
DESIRE

*Luxury, scandal, desire—welcome to
the lives of the American elite.*

Be transported to the worlds of oil barons, family dynasties,
moguls and celebrities. Get ready for juicy plot twists,
delicious sensuality and intriguing scandal.

6 NEW BOOKS AVAILABLE EVERY MONTH!

Get 4 FREE REWARDS!

We'll send you 2 FREE Books
plus 2 FREE Mystery Gifts.

Harlequin Desire books transport you to the world of the American elite with juicy plot twists, delicious sensuality and intriguing scandal.

FREE
Value Over
$20

YES! Please send me 2 FREE Harlequin Desire novels and my 2 FREE gifts (gifts are worth about $10 retail). After receiving them, if I don't wish to receive any more books, I can return the shipping statement marked "cancel." If I don't cancel, I will receive 6 brand-new novels every month and be billed just $4.55 per book in the U.S. or $5.24 per book in Canada. That's a savings of at least 13% off the cover price! It's quite a bargain! Shipping and handling is just 50¢ per book in the U.S. and $1.25 per book in Canada.* I understand that accepting the 2 free books and gifts places me under no obligation to buy anything. I can always return a shipment and cancel at any time. The free books and gifts are mine to keep no matter what I decide.

225/326 HDN GNND

Name (please print)

Address   Apt. #

City   State/Province   Zip/Postal Code

Email: Please check this box ☐ if you would like to receive newsletters and promotional emails from Harlequin Enterprises ULC and its affiliates. You can unsubscribe anytime.

Mail to the Harlequin Reader Service:
IN U.S.A.: P.O. Box 1341, Buffalo, NY 14240-8531
IN CANADA: P.O. Box 603, Fort Erie, Ontario L2A 5X3

Want to try 2 free books from another series? Call 1-800-873-8635 or visit www.ReaderService.com.

*Terms and prices subject to change without notice. Prices do not include sales taxes, which will be charged (if applicable) based on your state or country of residence. Canadian residents will be charged applicable taxes. Offer not valid in Quebec. This offer is limited to one order per household. Books received may not be as shown. Not valid for current subscribers to Harlequin Desire books. All orders subject to approval. Credit or debit balances in a customer's account(s) may be offset by any other outstanding balance owed by or to the customer. Please allow 4 to 6 weeks for delivery. Offer available while quantities last.

Your Privacy—Your information is being collected by Harlequin Enterprises ULC, operating as Harlequin Reader Service. For a complete summary of the information we collect, how we use this information and to whom it is disclosed, please visit our privacy notice located at corporate.harlequin.com/privacy-notice. From time to time we may also exchange your personal information with reputable third parties. If you wish to opt out of this sharing of your personal information, please visit readerservice.com/consumerschoice or call 1-800-873-8635. **Notice to California Residents**—Under California law, you have specific rights to control and access your data. For more information on these rights and how to exercise them, visit corporate.harlequin.com/california-privacy.

HD21R

Love Harlequin romance?

DISCOVER.

Be the first to find out about promotions,
news and exclusive content!

Facebook.com/HarlequinBooks

Twitter.com/HarlequinBooks

Instagram.com/HarlequinBooks

Pinterest.com/HarlequinBooks

ReaderService.com

EXPLORE.

Sign up for the Harlequin e-newsletter and
download a free book from any series at
TryHarlequin.com

CONNECT.

Join our Harlequin community to
share your thoughts and connect
with other romance readers!
Facebook.com/groups/HarlequinConnection